CLAW AND ORDER

MYSTIC NOTCH BOOK 8

LEIGHANN DOBBS

The book looked ancient. From its cracked leather binding to its brittle parchment-colored pages, the book exuded antiquity. It smelled ancient, too, giving off a slight whiff of vanilla mixed with something earthy and just a hint of mildew.

But even though it *looked* ancient, the printing was modern. The letters didn't have the flourish of an old printing press, and the ingredients listed didn't seem *that* old.

The recipes were a little usual. Grewel, wasters, and barley water weren't exactly modern fare. I flipped the pages carefully, and the letters swam before my eyes. I blinked, and they came back into focus. Yep, definitely not that old.

"A pretty good replica," I said as I flipped to the next page. Again, the letters seemed to transform before my eyes, and I squinted. The eye doctor had warned me that I would soon need reading glasses since I was in my late forties. I guessed the time had come. I made a mental note to make an eye doctor appointment.

"Mew!" Pandora, my cat, hopped up onto the counter. Every bookstore should have a cat, and Last Chance Books was no exception. I brought her to the store with me every day as my grandmother, who I'd inherited the shop and the cat from, had always done. Her sleek gray fur shone in the sunlight. She looked at me with reproachful, luminescent green eyes.

"What? It *is* a fake."

She twitched her tail, the slight kink on the end pointing toward the recipe section of the bookstore as if trying to tell me something.

"Yes, I know it's just a recipe book. Maybe it's just made to look old as a gimmick or something." I swear, the cat was almost human, and there were times when I actually thought she was trying to tell me something. But I also didn't need her bossing me around. Naturally, I knew it belonged in the cookbook section of the store. But not just yet. I had a list of people wanting to buy quirky cookbooks with old-fashioned recipes, and if I could sell this one without even putting it on the shelf, all the better.

I rummaged through the filing drawer under the counter, pulled out the list, and scanned the names.

Mary Ashford, Sonja Peterson, Danielle Norden, and—ugh—Felicity Bates. I had forgotten that my arch-nemesis had asked to be put on a list for recipe books months ago. She would be the last person I called. Hopefully one of the others would buy the book first. Maybe it was childish, but I secretly didn't want Felicity to have it, especially since I suspected she had designs on my boyfriend, Sheriff Eddie Striker.

"Speaking of Striker…" I glanced at the clock. It was almost time to meet him for our dinner picnic date.

"Merow?" Pandora brushed her cheek against the side of the box. Her eyes seemed a little brighter at the mention of Striker. I couldn't blame her. He had that effect on people—and cats.

"I'm going to dinner with Striker. Picnic in the park. You'll have to stay alone." I grabbed my purse, my brain conjuring up visions of cold fried chicken and wine atop a red-checked blanket on the grass.

Pandora purred and licked her paws innocently, which made me nervous. On a few occasions when I'd left her alone in the bookstore, I thought I'd seen her wandering around town. But it couldn't be. The store was locked, and there was no way for her to get out. Perhaps she had a doppelgänger.

I pulled the thick oak door open, flipped the closed sign, and took one last look at Pandora. She was lying on the counter, lazily twitching her tail as if to imply she was just going to lounge around in my absence, which made me very nervous.

My stomach grumbled, and I exited the shop, locking the door behind me. Hopefully, I wouldn't return to find that she'd spooled the toilet paper off the roll or thrown up a hairball on the purple micro-suede sofa. Her nonchalant demeanor on the counter gave me the feeling that something just wasn't right.

PANDORA JUMPED TO HER FEET AS SOON AS WILLA walked past the window, her auburn curls bouncing as she practically skipped toward her date with Striker.

The book! There was something about it. Something magical. Something she should pay attention to.

She couldn't blame Willa for not picking up on the special nature of the book. As one of the ancient cats of Mystic Notch, Pandora was privy to supernatural knowledge that mere humans could not fathom. She knew that there were certain relics hidden in town centuries ago, and if they fell into the wrong hands, Mystic Notch would not be the pleasant place it was now. Could the book be one of them?

"I told you there is a recipe for Robert Frosted Cookies in there." The ghost of Robert Frost materialized on the other side of the counter, and next to him, the ghost of Franklin Pierce. Yes, the ghosts of the poet and president haunted the bookstore. They were both from New Hampshire and had been haunting the bookstore since Willa's grandmother, Anna—Pandora's most beloved human—had owned it.

The ghosts were always feuding and playing pranks on the bookstore guests. Of course, no one could see them, but Willa could, and of course Pandora could also.

"That doesn't make you more important than me!" Franklin floated over and glared down at the book. "I bet they might have some Franklin Pierce Pies in there."

Robert Frost laughed. "You have miles to go before you find a book with a recipe named after you."

That was so like Robert, always working in a reference to one of his famous poems.

Franklin made a face. "I was president! People named many things after me!" He reached out for the book, managing to pick it up in his hand, which was unusual. Typically, the ghosts' hands went through solid matter. This was further evidence that the book was enchanted.

"Oh, look!" Franklin held the book up, and it opened on its own, magically flipping through the pages. A subtle lavender glow appeared around the edges. "I think I see a Franklin Pierce Pumpkin Bread recipe!"

"Let me see that." Robert grabbed the edge of the book in an attempt to wrestle it from Franklin.

"No, you don't!" Franklin pulled back.

"I just wanted to look." Robert tugged again.

Franklin jerked the book back.

Robert spun around. Cold goo splattered on Pandora's fur. She jumped back, shaking it off. Yuck.

Robert had grabbed the book mid-spin, and it flew out of Franklin's hand, bending at the spine. It hung in the air, balanced between Robert and Franklin's fingers.

And then it swiveled ninety degrees and shook itself. Something dropped out of it and clattered on the floor.

A fancy old skeleton key. And it was glowing.

The book thudded to the floor, no longer glowing. The key must have been giving it the magic. Robert and Franklin hovered over the book, their ghostly faces wrinkled in concern. But Pandora was more interested in the key. It must be a magical item. She needed to grab it and get it to the cats of Mystic Notch!

Pandora leapt down from the counter and pawed at the key. It was hot! Electricity zinged from her paw to her shoulder, and she jerked back.

Darn. That thing was dangerous. But she had to get it. If this was one of the items that could undo the pleasantry charm, she had to take it to the other cats so they could make sure it didn't fall into enemy hands.

"Oh dear, have we ruined it?" Robert swirled over the book, dripping cold, ghostly goo onto the pages.

"It will be ruined if you keep dripping on it!" Franklin swatted him out of the way.

Pandora didn't have time to get into the middle of their argument or worry about the book. The key was most important. She crouched over it, trying to come up with a plan to grab it.

Robert swirled over. "Hey, that looks like the key to my writing box!"

Pandora glanced up at him. "Your writing box?" That would be an odd coincidence, but stranger things had happened in the Notch.

"I had a lovely box I used to keep my poems in, and the key had a distinctive bow. That's the wide end, you know. Anyway, mine had a design just like this one with a notch on the top." Robert smiled at the key fondly. "The poems I put in that box always seemed to be my best sellers."

Pandora studied the key. It was very distinctive, with a fleur-de-lis inspired design, but surely there was more than one key with that design. Either way, she didn't have time for Robert's reminiscences.

She reached out tentatively with her paw and touched the bow end. That end was much less hot. Now all she had to do was pick it up securely with her mouth and use one of the escape routes to take it to the barn cats.

She touched it tentatively with her tongue.

Ping!

Willa's phone! Apparently, she'd been so intent on getting to her dinner with Striker, she'd left it on the counter. Pandora's nose wrinkled at the thought of the humans and their lovey-dovey machinations. It was distasteful, but they seemed happy, so she let them alone and ignored them when they got too friendly. She liked both Willa and Striker. In fact, it wouldn't be bad if they made a permeant alliance. What did humans call it? Marriage?

Wait, did she hear footsteps outside the door? She turned her attention back to the key, snaking out her paw and pushing at it. It had cooled off. She twitched her whiskers and picked the key up between her teeth.

"Oh-oh!" Franklin cast an alarmed look at the door and promptly disappeared.

"Trouble!" Robert yelled before fading out.

Shoot! The door creaked open.

Pandora's mind whirled. Willa would see the key sticking out of her mouth. She dropped it, and it clattered on the floor. She needed to bat it under something to hide it. The bookcases were too far. *The microsuede sofa.* If she swatted the key hard enough, and if she was lucky, it would slide just far enough under the sofa not to be noticeable from standing height and not come out the other side. She pulled her paw back.

"Pandora! What is this mess? Bad kitty!"

Too late.

Pandora plastered on a look of innocence and tried to make her sweetest, cutest face. She cocked her head and looked up at her human.

Willa's disappointed frown indicated that even her cutest face wasn't going to get her out of trouble.

Willa crouched down beside the book, and Pandora's heart fell at the crushed look in her amber eyes. Willa loved books, and Pandora knew seeing one damaged wounded her. She subtly moved her tail to cover the key. With any luck, Willa would be so intent on the book, she wouldn't notice the key.

"I guess it's not too bad." Willa picked the book up and then turned to Pandora. "Lucky thing for you it's not ruined."

Pandora felt better at that. Not that Willa would hand out a strict punishment, but it was punishment enough to disappoint her.

Willa stood and put the book on the counter. "Oh, there's my phone. Can't go far without that." She turned and held it up before putting it in her purse.

Pandora sat stock-still, trying to fluff out her tail to maximum width to hide the key. In her experience, humans were not that observant, so hopefully Willa would not notice the slight glow peeking out from between the hairs on her tail.

"Now you be a good—" Willa stopped midsentence and frowned at Pandora's tail. Darn!

Willa crouched down, and Pandora swished her tail, trying to push the key under the couch, but it was no use.

"Huh, look at that." Willa picked up the key and held it up. Oddly, it no longer glowed. Now it simply looked like a fancy brass skeleton key. "What an interesting key. I guess one of my customers must have dropped it. I'll just put it away for safekeeping."

Pandora hoped she would put it in the cash register drawer because she could easily open it and take the key out. But Pandora's hopes were dashed when Willa walked over to the tall shelf in the corner and took a box from the very top shelf. She opened the box and dropped the key inside.

"There. That should keep it safe." She started toward the door with a stern warning to Pandora. "Now, I'm going to enjoy my supper. You try to keep from destroying anything else in the store."

CHAPTER TWO

Striker had thought of everything as usual. The red-and-white-checkered cloth spread out on the grass was loaded with food, including a bucket of fried chicken, a bowl of potato salad, and a plate of peanut butter cookies. A bottle of wine wrapped in a red cloth was nestled in the old-fashioned wicker basket.

I plopped down next to him, my leg aching only slightly. The ache was a reminder of the accident that had sent me from my crime journalist job in Massachusetts up to the remote area of Mystic Notch, deep in the White Mountains of New Hampshire.

Striker topped off my wine glass and glanced around as he stashed the bottle back in the basket. "Hopefully your sister is busy at the station and won't come over and arrest us for public drinking."

My sister, Gus, was the town sheriff, and even

though we got along great, I wouldn't put it past her to arrest us. She did everything by the book, at least when she wasn't under some sort of enchantment spell. She wasn't one prone to showing favoritism to family.

I lowered my glass to avoid prying eyes. Striker was the sheriff of the next county, and it wouldn't be good for him to get arrested.

"I hope Pandora is okay alone in the shop. I had to go back to get my phone, and she'd knocked a book off the counter." I bit into a chicken leg. Crispy on the outside, juicy on the inside. Delicious.

"Never a dull moment with her," Striker said around a mouthful of potato salad.

"I found an old key too. She was practically sitting on it. I know it's silly, but I felt like she didn't want me to see it."

"Silly? I don't know. I think Pandora is more intelligent than most cats. No idea why she wouldn't want you to see a key, though."

"I know, right?" I had to admit, the cat did seem overly intelligent, but it was preposterous to think she'd be hiding a key from me. Yet there had been incidents in the past where I felt she was trying to tell me something.

"Then again, a lot of things are strange here in Mystic Notch." Striker gave me a pointed look.

I thought about the ghosts we could both see. Yeah, that's right. Striker and I could see ghosts. It had been happening to me since the aforementioned accident. I'd hid it from everyone except my best friend, Pepper St. Onge, who ran The Tea Shoppe in town. You can't imagine what a relief it was to discover that Striker could also see ghosts. Sometimes not the same ghosts, but still, it felt good to know I wasn't the only one and that I didn't have to keep secrets from him. Well, not that secret at least.

"True. At least Gus is back to normal."

Striker shook his head. "I'm not sure whether that's a good thing or bad thing."

I laughed. Gus was typically gung ho about law enforcement, but a recent hexing had turned her attitude from militant to lackadaisical. Thankfully, the hex had been reversed and things were back to normal. "And there are no deaths, so we won't have to deal with any ghosts popping up and demanding we investigate."

Ghosts could be pests, especially when they wanted their deaths avenged. It was doubly hard to accomplish that when we were trying to work around Gus, who had no idea ghosts existed.

"Maybe now we'll be able to spend more time focusing on us." Striker took my hand, his gray eyes looking into mine. My heart did a flip as I reached for another piece of fried chicken with my free hand.

It would be nice to have a break from ghosts and other odd things that seemed to happen frequently in Mystic Notch. I was curious and a little afraid to find out what "focusing on us" would entail. Even if I couldn't shake the ominous feeling that Pandora's odd behavior meant that this was just the calm before the storm.

PANDORA SAT IN HER CAT BED AND EYED THE BOX ON the top of the bookcase. She needed to get that key! Not that she hadn't tried. She'd leapt at the shelf, tried to climb up, and even attempted a risky jump from the filing cabinet. The box hadn't budged. Unfortunately, several other items on the bookcase had, and they now lay on the floor. Willa would not be pleased.

She sighed and turned three times in her fluffy cat bed that sat in a patch of sun on the sill of the large store window. Settling down, she wrapped her tail around her face and closed her eyes.

But just as she drifted into sleep, she felt an evil presence. Bolting up, she saw Felicity Bates and her villainous cat, Fluff, walking down the street.

Ugh. Fluff was the most objectionable of cats. He'd tried to harm the Mystic Notch cats many times and had almost succeeded in killing Pandora and Hope, the chimera cat that was magically powerful. If there was a side of good and a side of evil in Mystic Notch, Fluff was definitely on the side of evil, and so was his human, Felicity.

Where Fluff had tried to harm Pandora, Felicity had tried to harm Willa. Felicity fancied herself to be some sort of witch. With her long red hair and flowing dresses, she looked the part. Pandora didn't think she was very good at it, though, especially right now. She was walking a bit slowly, hunched over as she shuffled along. Her outfit was a little bland, with a dull-brown skirt and tan shirt. She did have a pair of nice Jimmy Choo sandals on. Maybe they hurt her feet and that was why she was shuffling. They didn't really go with the dress, but who was Pandora to judge.

Fluff trotted along a few steps in front of his mistress, his long white fur ruffling in the breeze. He swished his fluffy tail in the hair like a duster.

He turned and looked in Pandora's direction. She steeled herself for a telepathic battle of wills, but his gaze skipped right past her. Was he looking at the top shelf? Did he know about the key?

Pandora's worries increased. If Fluff was after the key, she really needed to get her act together and make sure she could deliver it to safe hands before Felicity or Fluff got ahold of it.

But how? She had to tell the Mystic cats about it, of course. They would just reinforce that she needed to get the key. And she'd probably have to listen to a bunch of criticism about how lacking she was in the ability to communicate with her human. Communicating with Willa wasn't as easy as it had been with

Anna, and the Mystic cats had been disappointed in Pandora's lack of progress in that area. The cats had a point though—if she were able to communicate, she could simply get Willa to give the key to Elspeth. But she'd tried so hard, and Willa seemed immune to cat telepathy. She'd had better luck getting through to Striker, but even then, she was only able to suggest simple things. There was no way she'd be able to communicate the importance of the key.

But luck might be on her side. The key had been well hidden in the book, and it was possible no one knew about it. If those with bad intent suspected that one of the relics had surfaced, they might think it was the book. Hadn't Willa said she had a waiting list for it? No doubt Felicity was on that list.

Hopefully the interested party would come for the book and not figure out the magical key hidden inside was no longer there. That might buy her some time.

Pandora cast another glance down the street. Good, Fluff and Felicity had walked on past and were a block down. She could rest now. She curled up in her cat bed, satisfied that the key was safe in its box for now. She'd have to pay attention though—if anyone came into the shop asking for it, she would have to act quickly.

CHAPTER THREE

"I shouldn't even let you come with me." I gave Pandora my sternest look. Given what she'd done to the old recipe book and the mess I'd found when I'd returned from my picnic with Striker, the cat was not in my good graces. But I didn't have the heart to forbid her from heading through the path in the woods to Elspeth's as was our usual routine. I knew how much she loved hanging around with the gaggle of cats Elspeth had in her barn.

I kind of liked the company. The woods could be a little scary at night, and I felt safer with Pandora by my side.

We started off down the path. It was still daylight, and squirrels rustled in the dry leaves on the forest floor. The low sun slanted through the woods, giving that golden glow that only happens just before sunset.

Elspeth was going out of town, and I wanted to drop off the basket of strawberry scones and special tea that Pepper had made for her before she left. I also wanted to check on her as I often did, since the elderly woman had been like a second grandmother to me. Elspeth and my own grandmother had been best friends their whole lives, thus the shortcut path through the woods between their houses. I'd traveled this path many times with my grandmother and Pandora, but now it was just the two of us. I glanced down at the cat, wondering if she missed my grandmother as much as I did. Probably. But I bet Pandora never trashed the bookstore when my grandmother had been in charge.

"I don't know what's gotten into you, but you need to stop wrecking the bookstore," I said.

"Meow!" Pandora didn't sound the least bit apologetic.

"No excuses either." I glanced down to see her attention was on a bird that had flown from a branch to the ground. "Maybe you need more exercise."

"Mew." She looked up at me, and I couldn't be sure, but I thought her reply might have been a bit sarcastic.

"Maybe I should stop giving you treats."

Hiss!

She didn't like that idea. "You've always been a good cat, so I'm going to overlook your behavior this time."

We came to the end of the path. Elspeth's mint-green Victorian with its pink gingerbread trim and roses twining along the porch railings came into view. Pandora gave me a short meow and trotted off toward the barn, leaving me to walk up to the porch and knock on Elspeth's door on my own.

In Elspeth's barn, the sun slanted in through the windows, leaving squares of golden light on the rough wood.

The barn was almost two hundred years old and still smelled of horses and hay. The floorboards creaked when humans stepped on them, but these days the barn was mostly inhabited by cats.

At first glance, one might think the ragtag gang of cats that Elspeth kept in her barn were strays, but they weren't. They were a magical breed of cat, tasked with keeping the balance of good and evil in Mystic Notch. Pandora was proud to be among their ranks.

As she entered, several cats stopped washing themselves and meowed a greeting.

Sasha, the Siamese, trotted over from where she'd been seated in front of the stainless steel food bowls, her sky-blue eyes brimming with curiosity.

Tigger, the striped cat who usually kept sentry on Elspeth's porch, stretched and trotted to join them.

Otis, the calico, looked down upon them from his perch in the loft. Being a male calico was rare, and Otis knew it, which was why he always acted so superior. But Pandora knew that deep down inside, he was really an old softie.

Inkspot, their leader, uncurled from his position in the corner and stretched, his jet-black fur sleek in the shadows. His wise green eyes assessed her.

"I sense there is a disturbance. Has another relic been found?" Inkspot's deep baritone filled the barn.

"A key was found hidden in an old recipe book in the bookstore," Pandora said.

"And where is it now?"

"Well… that's where there is a bit of a problem."

Several other cats had joined their circle. Snowball, with her long white fur; Hope, with her half-orange, half-black face; Kelley, the Maine Coon.

"Problem?" Sasha asked.

Pandora swallowed hard. Everyone was looking at her. "My human has hidden it out of reach."

"Hidden? Why?" Inkspot's eyes practically glowed. "Does she know that it's magical?"

"No." Pandora told them how it had fallen out of the recipe book and how she'd been caught trying to hide it under her tail. "Willa thought one of the customers might have dropped it, and she wanted to hold it for safekeeping."

"We need to get that key." Inkspot's tone was kind but firm.

Pandora looked down. "I know. I have a plan." Well, *sort of* a plan. Hopefully no one would ask for details.

Otis leapt down from the loft and trotted into the circle. "If you could only communicate with your human, you could simply ask her for it."

Pandora's fur bristled, and she resisted the urge to hiss at him. Leave it to Otis to act so condescending. She bit back a sarcastic reply, remembering that there was a time when Otis had risked his own life to save hers. She knew his bark was worse than his bite.

"I know, but she seems unwilling to receive my telepathic messages."

"Are you sure the problem is on her end?" Hope tilted her head. She was a chimera and looked like someone had taken two cats and mashed them together. Half of her face was black with a blue eye and the other half orange with a green eye. It looked unusual at any time, but even more so with her head tilted.

Pandora stared at her. She'd never considered that the communication problem wasn't on Willa's end. Willa was smart enough with regular things, but she was a little slow on the uptake with the magical properties of Mystic Notch. And since Pandora had been able to communicate with Willa's grandmother Anna perfectly, she'd just assumed the problem was with Willa. But what if it wasn't?

"What do you mean?" Pandora asked.

"Well, I know that you had good communication with her predecessor," Hope said.

"I did indeed." Pandora's heart squeezed at the thought of Anna. She'd loved her very much. Of course, she loved Willa, too, but Anna had been "the one."

"And you are still attached to your prior human?"

"Yes. Well, Anna is gone, but I will never forget her."

"Then have you considered that maybe your love for Anna is what's holding you back? Maybe you are afraid that communicating with Willa won't be as satisfying or that in some way it diminishes what you had with Anna."

"I hadn't really thought about that." *Could that be true?*

Hope shrugged. "Might be something to consider."

Otis swished his tail. "This psychoanalysis is all very touchy-feely, but you need to get the key however you can."

"I tried the usual methods of knocking the box off the shelf," Pandora said. "Didn't work. It's too high on the shelf. But I'm going to keep my eye on it, of course. If Willa tries to give it to anyone, I'll get it somehow."

"This does not bode well. Keys usually open something." Hope looked concerned.

"You mean it could be a device to unlock a portal?" Sasha asked.

"I hope not, but we must keep it in mind."

Otis shook his head. "No one in their right mind would open a portal. It's dangerous."

"Unless you have the instructions," Hope pointed out.

All the cats nodded. There had been instructions, but the cats had protected them by burying them in a place where they were safe from humans. At least, they thought they would be safe.

"We'd better make sure the instructions are still where we buried them in Gladys Primble's yard," Inkspot said. "Otis, are you still in communication with Euphoria?"

Euphoria was Gladys Primble's cat, a gorgeous Selkirk Rex with unusual curly hair. Pandora thought that Otis might have had something going on with her at one time, but she hadn't seen her around lately. Perhaps it was only a passing infatuation.

Otis nodded. "I am. She hasn't mentioned a breach."

"Good. Then you will be in charge of making sure the instructions remain intact." Inkspot scanned the group. "The rest of us must remain vigilant."

"You said the key was in the book?" Sasha asked. "Then maybe we need to be wary of the person who comes for the book. They might not know it no longer holds the key."

Inkspot washed behind his ear. "That may be a lucky break. Perhaps we can resolve this problem by dealing with the one who seeks the book."

Otis nodded. "Head it off at the pass, so to speak?"

"Yes." Inkspot turned to Pandora. "It's of the utmost importance that you watch for this person. And please try to retrieve the key. If there was ever a time to step up your efforts to communicate with Willa, it would be now."

The next morning, I parked my Jeep in the town lot, and Pandora and I trotted down to open Last Chance Books. Pandora had seemed a little down after we'd gotten back from Elspeth's the previous night. Maybe I'd been too hard on her after coming back from my dinner with Striker and finding the shop in shambles. I'd try to be nicer to her today.

The regulars were waiting at the door with coffees. I'd "inherited" the four senior citizens along with the bookstore. They'd been gathering first thing in the morning at Last Chance Books with my grandmother for decades, and the tradition continued after I inherited it.

One of the regulars, Bing Thorndike, held a tray with coffee for all of us. The prospect of a coffee had me quickening my pace.

"Good morning, Willa," Hattie Deering said. She

and her twin sister, Cordelia, were dressed in summery outfits. Hattie wore a flowered peach top and yellow polyester pants, and Cordelia wore a flowered yellow top and peach polyester pants. The two had been dressing in coordinating outfits ever since they were toddlers, and it always amused me to see what they were wearing.

"Morning! Hope you are all well today."

They stepped aside so I could open the door, and Josiah bent down to pet Pandora. He was pretty spry for an eighty-year-old, but I supposed that being the town mail carrier had kept him in good shape.

I pushed the door open, and we all went in. Pandora trotted straight to her cat bed in the window, and the others settled on the sofa and chairs I kept for readers to use if they wanted to settle in with a book.

"Here's your coffee, Willa." Bing handed me a cup, and I flipped the plastic lid. His blue eyes sparkled with life, as usual. Bing was always happy and kindly and had a magical quality about him. Not surprising, since he'd been a magician his entire life.

"Your hair looks nice, both of you," I told Hattie and Cordelia. The two women spent an inordinate amount of time at the local hair salon, The Cut & Curl. I thought it was mostly for the gossip, but today they were sporting newly updated hairstyles, and the color looked to be a brighter white than usual.

Cordelia patted the side of her hair. "Thank you. Myra outdid herself."

"Makes you look years younger," Josiah said. "Both of you."

Hattie waved her hand. "Oh, go on. A new hairstyle is always so refreshing. Too bad Myra couldn't make Felicity Bates look younger."

"Or act nicer," Cordelia added.

My gut churned at the mention of my nemesis, but I was curious. "Why? What's up with Felicity?"

"Well, you didn't hear it from me, but she looks a bit ragged." Hattie sipped her coffee.

"And that disagreement she had with Sarah Delaney was rather outrageous," Cordelia said.

Bing leaned forward. I hadn't realized he was so interested in town gossip. "Disagreement?"

"They were getting their nails done and were seated beside each other. Sarah was so mad she slammed down her hand, and nail tips went everywhere."

I looked self-consciously at my own chipped, unpolished nails. Maybe it was time I scheduled a manicure. Perhaps after my eye doctor appointment.

"It was a terrible row, but I'm not sure what it was about," Hattie said.

Cordelia pressed her lips together. "My memory is a little fuzzy, but I believe it had something to do with pumpkin bread."

"Pumpkin bread?" Josiah looked confused.

Cordelia nodded. "Yes, they were arguing about what spices to use. Very weird."

I glanced over at the old recipe book that still sat on the counter. Coincidence? I wondered. Felicity's name was on that list. All the more reason to make sure someone *else* on the list got the book. I made a mental note to call Mary Ashford as soon as the regulars left.

"And it wasn't just them," Hattie piped in. "Josie Martin egged them on."

"Probably trying to get a story for the paper. I hear that she is running out of things to write about," Cordelia said.

Josie Martin worked for the Mystic Notch Gazette. I wasn't surprised she might be looking for stories. Not much happened in our small town.

"They did a big article on A Good Yarn last month." Hattie's expression registered disapproval. "I thought they might be trying to capitalize on the big brouhaha with Jack McDougal's murder."

Jack had been the proprietor of Jack's Cards, a store that sold collectible trading cards. Mrs. Quimby, the proprietor of A Good Yarn, the yarn shop across the street from Jack's, had been briefly involved in the case.

"I wouldn't put it past her," Josiah said. "But I play chess with Ed Granger, and he did mention something about the Gazette doing pieces on local shops. I guess that's what papers do when there isn't much interesting news."

"Maybe they'll do one on the bookstore," Bing said to Willa.

"Maybe." The store did well, and I didn't really need a write-up, but I supposed it couldn't hurt. As long as Franklin and Robert didn't decide to add some interest to the article by playing one of their pranks.

"Well, I have to get going to the Elks lodge." Bing stood and stretched, and the others followed, stopping to deposit their cups in the trash.

"You haven't noticed anything unusual lately, have you, Willa?" Bing's question caught me off guard. He'd asked me that before, and I always thought it was kind of weird.

I glanced over at Pandora. She had ruined a book and trashed the store. She'd never done that before. "Pandora has been acting a bit funny."

Everyone frowned and looked over at the cat, who was fast asleep in her bed.

"I hope she's not under the weather," Hattie said.

"Maybe you should take her to the vet," Cordelia added.

"She does need a checkup. But other than that, nothing unusual has happened. Why do you ask?" I looked up at Bing, who simply shrugged.

"Oh, no reason. Just wanted to make sure things were back to normal after Jack's murder."

They filed out of the shop. It was nice of Bing to

check, and I was glad things were back to normal. Or were they?

A visit to the veterinarian!

Pandora's fur bristled at the thought. She'd been lying in half slumber, listening to the conversation with one eye slitted open, watching the box that held the key.

She was not amused by the suggestion that she needed to see the veterinarian. She hated going there. She was grateful that the doctor had saved her life the time the bookcase fell on her, but still. She disliked needles and how they stuck that thermometer in places where nothing should be stuck. She'd better be on her best behavior so that Willa would stop entertaining any thoughts of taking her to the vet.

But now, she needed to try to communicate with her human.

Pandora stood and made a show of stretching.

"Ah, feeling better?" Willa petted her, concern brimming in her amber eyes.

"Meow." Pandora purred.

"Good."

Pandora focused her attention on her human, trying to telepath one thought.

Get the box.

"Hm. Now, what was I going to do?" Willa

turned, slowly surveying the room, her gaze stopping at the shelf.

Yes! Move the box closer, Pandora telepathed.

"I was going to move something," Willa said.

Yes! Yes! The box, the box, the box!

Willa snapped her fingers. "The clock! Yes. Hm. Now, where did I want to move that?"

She headed toward the clock on the wall next to the shelf and lifted it off, then turned and surveyed the room.

Darn! Maybe something simpler would be better. Pandora's gaze fell on the coffee cup.

Sip coffee.

Willa hung the clock on the wall behind the sofa and stood back. "Perfect! Looks much better there."

She turned and walked back behind the counter, hesitating as she passed her coffee cup.

Pandora held her breath as Willa reached out for the cup.

"This is probably cold." She took the cup to the small kitchenette in the back, and Pandora could hear her tossing the liquid down the sink.

Did that count? Willa had thought about drinking the coffee, right?

Pandora wasn't sure. She sighed and sat back in the bed, glaring up at the box. How in the world was she going to get that key?

The door opened, and Willa's best friend, Pepper St. Onge, bounced in. Her long red hair was piled high atop her head, and she held a quilted bag that she carried her tea supplies in. Pepper owned a shop in town called The Tea Shoppe and was always making some sort of herbal tea concoction.

Pepper thought her tea had magical powers, but Pandora had only ever seen those concoctions backfire. Hopefully, the tea she had in her bag now wasn't charmed with anything, or there could be unpredictable consequences for Willa.

Willa came out from the back. "Hey, Pepper."

"Hey, yourself." Pepper pointed to her bag. "Do you have time for a break? I brought some tea and scones, and I have a favor to ask."

Pepper pulled a mason jar out of her bag. Golden liquid swirled inside. "I'm trying a new tea with special properties."

Pepper sounded enthusiastic, but Pandora thought she sensed Willa doing a mental eye roll. Willa had been the victim of Pepper's tea-with-special-properties before.

Willa held her hands up in front of her. "I'm not up for any special tea right now."

"It's not for you. It needs to steep in sunshine for three days, and your window faces south. I don't have any good windows for it in my shop, and besides, I'm going away to an herbal convention."

"A convention? That sounds fun."

Pepper rolled her eyes. "Hardly. A bunch of would-be herbalists trying to one-up each other.

Lots of drama." Pepper handed the jar of tea to Willa.

Willa glanced at the window. "I'll just put this in the corner away from the cat bed. Pandora won't mind sharing, will you?"

Pandora wasn't sure. It looked like it wouldn't take up too much space, so she supposed she could make do.

Willa placed the jar on the window. Apparently, she wasn't going to wait for an answer.

"What does the tea do?" Willa asked as they got settled in the chairs. Pepper unpacked her bag. Green tea, strawberry scones, and—yum—milk. She hoped it was full fat and not that two-percent crap.

Pandora trotted over and rubbed against Pepper's leg.

Pepper was too excited about her tea to pay attention to Pandora like she usually did. She leaned forward, her green eyes bright, as she talked to Willa. "This is my best one yet. It removes emotional blockers that are getting in people's way. It's very important."

Pandora watched as Pepper poured a splash of milk into her tea and willed her to put some in a saucer for Pandora like she usually did.

Willa made a face. "Blockers? What do you mean?"

Who cares! Pandora wanted a saucer of milk. Didn't Pepper realize that?

"You know, like if you have some hang-up that keeps you from moving forward. For example, let's say you wanted to get closer to Striker, but the emotional baggage from your old divorce was holding you back from committing. That sort of thing."

"Is that what you think is going on with me?" Willa sounded incredulous.

Pandora stood on her hind legs to see whether Pepper had put the saucer of milk on the table and perhaps forgotten to move it to the floor for Pandora. Nope.

"No. That was just an example." Pepper sat back and sipped. "Why, is it?"

"No. I don't have any emotional baggage blocking me. Things are going fine with Striker." Willa took a scone from the dainty china plate. "I think Pandora is looking for her saucer of milk."

Finally! If it were anything else, Pandora might have had a glimmer of hope that her telepathy with Willa was improving, but she knew there was no need to read her mind when it came to giving her a saucer of milk.

CHAPTER FIVE

Try as I might to not think about it, my gaze kept straying to the tea Pepper had put in the window. Was it some kind of hint? I rarely thought of my ex-husband. It had been years. And I didn't think I had any emotional baggage that was holding me back from Striker. Maybe Pepper simply did want a sunny window, and mine fit the bill. That's why Pandora liked it so much.

"I think I'm reading too much into this tea," I said.

"Meumphhh." Pandora gave a half meow, half purr, which I took as agreement.

"You think so too? Good. I should get back to putting these books away."

Turning from the cat, a thought nagged at me. *The key!* I'd put it in the box and should try to find the owner. *Should I make a flyer? Maybe just ask people? Or wait for someone to claim it?*

I was trying to decide when the door opened, and Mary Ashford entered. She was the first name on the list for unique recipe books, and I'd called her after Pepper left.

"Hi, Willa. Do you have the book?" Mary was younger than me, probably mid-thirties. She was tall, with shoulder-length jet-black hair and eager dark eyes. She looked like she really wanted the book. Good. I was happy to sell it to her and avoid having to call Felicity Bates.

"Right here." I pushed the book, which was still on the counter, toward her.

"It's gorgeous." She ran her hands over the cover then opened it. I looked on as she paged through the recipes, squinting, which reminded me about the eye appointment I'd booked.

"It's in very good condition," I said. *Especially considering it was knocked on the floor.*

"How old do you think it is?" Mary looked up at me.

"Not as old as it looks. The cover and paper are made to look old, I think. But the typing seems more modern."

She frowned at me as if she didn't understand. I was sure I was right. My eyes weren't that bad.

"Some of the recipes look old, though," I said.

"Okay, great. I'll take it. I'm putting together a series of antique recipes for my cooking blog."

"These should fit the bill." I rang her up, and she left the shop, clutching the bag with the book inside as if it were the most precious thing on earth.

"Mew!" Pandora had hopped on the counter while Mary was looking at the book and had been watching us intently. Now she was staring at me. Maybe she needed a treat.

I fished some of her favorite salmon nuggets out of a drawer, and she gobbled them up just as Striker came in. He was dressed in his brown sheriff uniform, and filled it out quite nicely, I might add.

My heart smiled at the sight of him, but my eyes couldn't keep from sliding over to the tea.

"Hey." He came over and kissed me on the forehead.

"Hi!" *Did I sound over-exuberant?* Darn it, that tea was making me act weird.

"Meow." Pandora raced over to Striker and rubbed against his ankles. He bent down to pet her.

"How are my favorite girls today?" he asked, mostly to Pandora.

"Great. Had a visit from Pepper already and sold a book from that estate sale I went to this weekend. How about you?"

"It's quiet today, and I was just dropping off some paperwork to Gus, so I figured I'd swing in."

It felt good that Striker always stopped in when he was in town. Even though he was the sheriff of the neighboring county, he and Gus often consulted on cases since staffing was low in our small part of the world. Now that he was here, it didn't seem like he thought anything was lacking or that I had some baggage that was stopping me from moving forward in our relationship. Pepper had psyched me out with that tea, and I was reading things into it that weren't there.

"Anyway, I gotta run, but I wanted to stop in and see if you wanted me to bring anything for dinner tonight."

Striker knew me too well and knew that I would only have crackers and cottage cheese in my kitchen.

"Pizza?" It was our favorite.

"You got it. I better get a move on." He gave me a brief kiss on the lips. Brief but exciting, nonetheless.

I watched him leave, wondering whether there really was something off with our relationship or if it was all my imagination brought on by Pepper's tea.

PANDORA LICKED A FEW SMALL CRUMBS FROM THE salmon treat off her whiskers as she thought about Mary Ashford buying the book. Was Mary the person who wanted the relic to destroy Mystic Notch? Pandora hadn't felt a malicious vibe from her, but many of her foes were adept at hiding their true intentions.

Mary had said she wanted old recipes for her cooking blog. Perhaps that was her only interest in the book. If that were the case, someone else out there was going to be pretty upset that Mary had that cookbook.

Still, she couldn't rule out that Mary was the person who wanted the key. She needed to alert the cats right away. If Willa left the shop today, she'd make a sneaky visit to the barn. Pandora had an escape route that Willa was unaware of, and if she timed it right, she could make her visit and get back before Willa even suspected she was gone. She'd been smart enough to periodically take catnaps in strange places so that Willa would simply assume she was tucked away in one of her corners if she came back and Pandora wasn't in her cat bed in the window.

If Willa didn't leave, she could always sneak out tonight when Willa and Striker were focused on their pizza.

Either way, she had a long wait, so she settled into her cat bed and was in a deep sleep when she was rudely awakened by someone shouting.

"You had no right to sell that! I had dibs!"

The screeching voice belonged to Danielle Norden. She was standing on the opposite side of the counter from Willa, her fists clenched at her sides. Her face was red with anger.

"I'm sorry, Danielle, but Mary was on the list ahead of you because she asked first." Willa remained calm. Pandora had to give her credit. If anyone spoke to Pandora like that, she'd arch her back and give them the full power of her hiss. Of course, Willa couldn't exactly do that.

Danielle's beady eyes narrowed. "Let me see the list."

Willa looked around on the counter. "I think I threw it out after Mary picked up the book. No need for it. How did you even know I had an old-looking cookbook?"

"Hattie mentioned it at the Cut & Curl."

"Well, I'm sorry, but Mary really did ask for it first."

Danielle crossed her arms over her chest. "You expect me to believe that? Well, I certainly will never shop here again!"

She spun around and stormed off.

"Jeez, what is wrong with her? That was a tad bit of an overreaction, don't you think?" Willa turned to Pandora.

Pandora didn't think so, but of course Willa couldn't understand her reply no matter how hard she worked to get the message across.

If Danielle wanted the book because of its magical contents, then her reaction to finding out Mary had it didn't seem out of place. But was that the reason? And did Mary want it for its magical powers, or did she just want an old cookbook?

Pandora didn't know the answer, but one thing was clear. If Mary or Danielle knew about the magic, they apparently didn't realize that the key was no longer in the book.

Pandora glanced at the box with the key. At least it was safe and sound.

"I guess I'll put these away. I have an eye doctor appointment tomorrow, so I want to finish stocking the books before we leave." Willa picked up a pile of books and disappeared into the shelves.

Pandora curled up in her bed beside Pepper's tea, which was now turning an ominous murky brown. A sense of foreboding settled in. If only she could tell Willa about the key. At least two people were after the book, and she couldn't help but feel that things were going to heat up.

If only Robert and Franklin would appear. Maybe Pandora could have them pass the message to Willa. But they were nowhere to be seen.

Pandora sighed and tucked her nose under her tail. At least she could tell the cats of these new developments. Hopefully, they would come up with a plan.

CHAPTER SIX

Striker arrived with the pizza that night right on time. It was green pepper and onion, one of my favorites. He got some plates from the cabinet while I spooled paper towels off the roll on the counter. He went into the small bathroom off the kitchen to wash his hands.

"The bathrooms are so small in this place. Good thing it's only you."

Was that some kind of hint? "They are? I guess they weren't into big bathrooms back in Victorian times. Since it was only Gram here, it didn't matter."

"Yeah. Perfect for one, but if you had another person here, it might be hard to keep all your stuff like toothbrushes and all the things girls have on the sink."

Okay, that was definitely a hint. And he had a point. The bathrooms were small, and I wouldn't mind more space for myself. I made a mental note to talk to Steve Wheeler about what could be done to expand the bathrooms. Maybe he could even rip out the smaller bedroom upstairs and make it an en suite bath for the master.

But in the meantime, should I offer to clear off some space on the small surface of the sink? Maybe even get a toothbrush holder so that he could keep his here? Mine was taking up a lot of space just lying there on the sink in the upstairs bathroom.

Striker picked up the plates, napkins, and pizza box and gestured toward the living room where we usually lounged in front of the TV on pizza night. "You want to eat in there?"

"Of course."

We got settled on the couch and were just digging in to the first slice when Pandora appeared out of nowhere and jumped onto the coffee table.

"She does love her pizza." Striker broke off a tiny bit of crust and fed it to her.

"Meow!" She stared at us as if trying to tell us something.

"I think she wants more pizza, but I don't want to feed her too much. I'm not sure it's good for them."

Pandora flopped onto her side on the table and stared at the pizza. If a cat could look exasperated, she was doing a good job.

I munched my slice, feeling guilty, and watched as she snaked her silvery paw out to touch the crystal paperweight that Elspeth had given me when I moved in.

Pandora had always had an attraction to the thing, and it was no wonder. Even though it was just plain glass, it displayed the most gorgeous rainbow of colors, and the upside-down reflections of the room almost looked like scenes sometimes. I had to confess, there were a few times when I thought I'd seen something more in there, but I doubted that was possible. Even if I was starting to believe there might be more to Mystic Notch than met the eye, it was a little far-fetched to think there was magic in my paperweight.

"How was your day?" Striker's question pulled my attention from the paperweight, which had had a mesmerizing effect on me.

"Pretty good. I sold that old cookbook to Mary Ashford, and then Danielle Norden came in looking for it and had a meltdown."

Striker's left brow quirked up. "Over a cookbook?"

"Yeah." I snorted. "Can you believe that?"

"Mew!" Pandora sounded outraged, too, but maybe that was because she wanted another bite of pizza.

She pushed the paperweight precariously close to the edge of the table.

"Careful with that. That was a gift from Elspeth, and I don't want to break it." I pushed it back into the middle.

Pandora stared at me with those golden-green eyes as if she wanted to sass me back. She pushed the paperweight toward me.

"Okay, enough. I'll give you another little bite of crust, but no sauce. It's too salty." I pinched off a tiny bit, and she gobbled it up. I turned my attention back to the problem with Striker. How should I go about offering him a toothbrush spot? Was it too presumptuous? If Pepper had brought that tea over as a hint for me because she knew something I didn't, then it probably wasn't.

"What about you? Did you have a good day?" I asked him. "I appreciate you coming all the way from Dixford Pass." Striker lived about thirty minutes away, and it was nice that he always came to my place for my convenience.

"It's no problem. My place is too small. My day was uneventful. Just doing paperwork, and I had to drop some lab results off for Gus, so I was in town anyway." Striker picked up another slice. "Plus, you have better pizza here."

"Meow!" The mention of pizza had Pandora riled up again, and she batted the paperweight.

I sighed and watched her push it around as she looked from me to the pizza to the paperweight.

"What is wrong with her tonight? She seems unsettled." Striker said.

"Beats me. Maybe she's getting spoiled."

"Meow!" Pandora shot her paw out and whacked

the paperweight. It fell to the floor and rolled under the couch. Thankfully, it stayed on the oriental throw rug and didn't shatter.

I wagged my finger at the cat. "Acting like a spoiled brat is not going to get you another piece of pizza."

PANDORA MEOWED WITH FRUSTRATION AS SHE HOPPED down from the coffee table and watched the paperweight roll around under the couch. Willa did not understand a thing she'd been trying to tell her.

Yes, she did like pizza, but that wasn't the thought she had been trying to get across to the humans. Not only had her meows been misinterpreted, but if Willa had any bit of a telepathic acumen, she would have seen there was a message in the miniature crystal ball that Willa thought was a paperweight.

Except now, the only image she could see was a toothbrush. What was up with that?

Willa and Striker had gone on talking about their day, completely unaware of the importance of Pandora's message.

Pandora went back to staring at the pizza. She was in a rush to get to the barn and tell the cats about what had happened in the bookstore. She'd have to wait the humans out, but it wouldn't be long before they went upstairs, and she could escape through her secret exit in the basement.

In one way, she dreaded going to the barn. She knew the cats, especially Otis, would be disappointed with her lack of communication with Willa. Hopefully, there were still things they could do to protect the key even without Willa's help.

And if she ever *was* able to talk to Willa, she was going to speak to her about how stingy they were with the pizza. A couple of tiny crumbs of crust just didn't cut it.

THREE HOURS LATER, PANDORA WAS FINALLY AT Elspeth's barn. She wondered why she'd been in such a hurry to get to the cats. As predicted, they were not pleased with her lack of communication with her human.

"So, we have two suspects, then. Mary Ashford and Danielle Norden." Inkspot sat in the shaft of light from a moonbeam that filtered in from the high window on the side of the barn.

"It would seem that way." Pandora had told them about Mary and Danielle being on the list and Danielle's reaction to the news that Willa had sold the book to Mary.

"At least that gives us a start." Snowball's white

fur gave her the appearance of a ghost in the dim light.

"And you're sure the key is still safe?" Otis looked down at her condescendingly from atop a bale of hay.

"Yes, it's still safe. I've kept my eye on it at all times, and no one has been in the shop when I wasn't there." Pandora refrained from rolling her eyes. Did Otis think she was an amateur?

Inkspot turned to Tigger. "Have you verified the instructions are still where we left them?"

Otis nodded. "Euphoria will keep watch, and I will take a few shifts to help her out."

"Okay, then. Pandora, you continue to keep an eye on the key. Tigger, Hope, and Sasha will go on a recon mission to sniff out what Mary Ashford and Danielle Norden are up to," Inkspot said.

"There is more than just those two." Kelley the Maine Coon came out of the shadows. She resembled a lion with her long, striped fur. "I've heard that Felicity Bates and Sarah Delaney have an interest in the book."

Snowball hissed. "Oh no. If those two are involved, that does not bode well."

"Never mind them, what about Fluff?" Hope asked. There was no love lost between Hope and Fluff since he had once tried to burn Hope—and Pandora—alive.

"If Felicity is involved, you know Fluff has to be as well," Otis said.

"That one is not to be trusted." Hope warned. "And don't forget his human has charms and spells. You must be aware at all times. One sleep charm, and they can sneak past you without you ever knowing."

"All the more reason for everyone to be on their toes." Inkspot turned to Pandora. "It would be of the utmost help if you could *finally* communicate with Willa. We need to secure that key at all costs. If Felicity and Sarah really are involved, the results could be disastrous."

CHAPTER SEVEN

"Stupid reading glasses." I shoved the prescription into my purse and pulled out of the vision center parking lot. At least the tortoise-shell frames I'd picked out looked cute on me and complemented my copper curls. But I hated the idea of having to root around in my purse for a pair of glasses every time I wanted to read the fine print.

Was it only a matter of time before I needed them to read books? Right now, I could see the letters on most books, though I had caught myself looking for large-print editions more often. Reading was my life, and it would be inconvenient to have to fiddle with glasses at night. Maybe I should have gotten two pairs so I could leave one beside the bed. Or maybe I would get an e-reader and adjust the print size.

I parked in the town lot and started toward the bookstore with a tingle of trepidation. I'd dropped

Pandora off at the store before my appointment, and I shuddered to think about what havoc she might have wreaked. I got the impression she was still mad about the pizza. Had she spooled the toilet paper across the store? Maybe she'd coughed up a hairball in some hidden spot that I would only find through the disgusted yelp of a customer.

The fact that she hadn't minded being left in there alone raised my suspicions. And she'd been acting weird lately, always looking at the shelves behind the cash register. She'd climbed on them and knocked things off too. Visions of the shelves on the ground and a squished cat underneath them bubbled up.

I picked up the pace and rounded the corner, my heart jolting at what I saw. A flap of a black dress disappeared around the corner into the alley beside my shop. *Sarah Delaney!*

Had she been at my shop? I glanced at the door. There was no note. The door looked fine. But why was she running away down the alley?

I ran to the alley, but she was already gone. Darn, she was fast. Must have already disappeared out the other end. Weird behavior, to be sure, but Sarah was known for being weird.

The thick oak door to Last Chance Books was still locked, but I felt tension as I opened it to find…

Nothing amiss.

Pandora was fast asleep in her cat bed. The

shelves had not been destroyed, and no toilet paper was strewn about.

I'd let my imagination run away with me.

Pandora raised her head and blinked at me from her cat bed.

"Guess it's been quiet here? No one tried to break in?" I asked her even though I knew she wouldn't answer. Sometimes I wished she would. She'd probably be a good conversationalist, and it did get lonely in the shop during the quiet times.

"Mew." Pandora's eyes narrowed, and she looked at the shelves again. Just what was her obsession with those things?

PANDORA BLINKED AT WILLA. HAD SHE JUST SAID someone had been trying to break in? Her question was answered as Willa continued to ramble.

"I thought I saw someone run down the alley. Flowing black dress, long black hair flying behind it. Could only be one person—Sarah Delaney."

Pandora practically fell out of her cat bed. Sarah Delaney? Here? She hadn't sensed a nefarious presence. She'd been sound asleep. Maybe Willa was mistaken. She did just come from the eye doctor, and perhaps her vision was impaired.

Pandora glanced at the box on the shelf. It wasn't possible that Sarah could have broken in and stolen the key right under Pandora's nose. But if she'd done something magically... Sarah was a witch and might be able to open the shop door with a spell. And then if she'd somehow hexed Pandora with a sleep charm...

This was not good. Not good at all.

Willa appeared unconcerned as she straightened the pillows on the purple sofa and chairs and dusted the coffee table and side tables.

"I missed the regulars and my coffee this morning. I suppose I'll have to suffer with the coffee from the K-Cup machine in back."

Forget about the coffee and think about the key! Pandora screamed at Willa inside her head.

But Willa didn't even turn to look at her. It was as if her telepathic attempts were blocked.

Pandora's attention was drawn to the tea next to her bed. The sunlight was filtering through the liquid, giving it a golden glow. It looked welcoming and inviting.

She remembered Otis's words about the problem being with Pandora and not Willa. What if that were true? She had had a special bond with Anna. What if she had subconsciously blocked herself from having that same bond with anyone else?

And if Sarah *had* been here, maybe it was time to do something drastic.

Pepper had said the tea would help with blocked communications.

Pandora flipped open the latch to the top, and the jar popped open. Pepper's teas were known for backfiring, but she had to take a chance. She was desperate. She braced herself for the worst, then stuck her head in and started drinking.

It wasn't too bad, actually. Kind of like honey and moss with a tinge of licorice. How much should she drink? Would there be adverse effects if she drank too much?

She drank as fast as she could. As the level of liquid went down, she stuck her head in farther.

"Pandora! No!"

Through the inside of the jar, Pandora saw Willa racing over. The curve of the glass distorted the panicked look on Willa's face, making it almost comical. She reached out, her hand appearing huge as it came toward Pandora.

Pandora jerked her head out, and the glass tipped. The rest of the liquid spilled on the windowsill before the jar rolled off and shattered on the floor.

Pandora lapped up the rest of the liquid that had spilled on the windowsill.

Willa was looking down at her in horror.

"What have you done?"

Pandora opened her mouth to answer, but all that came out was…

"Burp!" Pandora grimaced. "Err… sorry."

Willa gestured to the mess on the floor. "You better be sorry!

Willa started toward the closet where they kept the broom and dustpan. She stopped midway and slowly turned to stare at Pandora. "Wait a minute. Did you just *talk*?"

CHAPTER EIGHT

*A*pparently, the coffee that Bing and the others usually brought was vital for my sanity because I could have sworn I just heard Pandora speak words. Human words.

"Yep, it's me talking to you. We can communicate!" Pandora seemed overjoyed.

I, on the other hand, was terrified. Maybe it had something to do with those drops they'd put in my eyes at the optometrist. I blinked and shook my head.

"You're not seeing things, or hearing things." Pandora twitched her tail. "We can communicate. My meows are actual words to you now. Pepper's tea helped."

My gaze switched to the broken mason jar. "You mean, you drank this tea, and now I can hear you in words?"

"Yes! Exactly! Isn't that what I just said?" Pandora

trotted over to the broom closet. "Now, let's clean it up, I don't want to get a sliver of glass in my paw. We have a lot to catch up on."

I'll say. Pandora watched as I cleaned up the glass. I couldn't exactly ask her to help. She couldn't hold a broom, and from what I'd experienced with her before we could communicate, she wasn't the type that cleaned up.

"So, Pepper's teas really are magic?" I asked.

"I guess, but they mostly backfire, as you know."

Did I ever. "And there's magic here in town. Or at least a magical cat?"

The idea of magic existing in Mystic Notch wasn't new to me. After all, I did have two ghosts in the bookstore that I had regular conversations with, not to mention the dozens that had appeared wanting me to solve murders. There had also been a few incidents that defied logical explanation, so maybe talking to my cat wasn't that far-fetched.

"There's more than one magical cat. All the cats over at Elspeth's are magical. You see, we're descended from a long line of cats that are sworn to keep Mystic Notch from falling into evil ways."

That sounds a bit overdramatic, I thought as I emptied the dustbin full of glass into the trash. "Does Elspeth know about her cats?"

"You betcha. She's got some skills herself."

I stared at my cat. Was she saying that the kindly white-haired lady I thought of as a second grandmother was some sort of witch? I really needed that coffee.

"Wait, you *talk* to Elspeth?" I headed toward the back room where the Keurig machine was. Pandora padded along beside me.

"Tigger is the one that has the telepathic connection to Elspeth, so he does most of the talking. Of course, she does address us and ask us to do things." Pandora started grooming herself while I made the coffee. "Oh, and you know that paperweight she gave you when you inherited the house?"

"Yeah?"

"It's not a paperweight."

So I *had* seen images in there. "Let me guess. It's some sort of crystal ball?"

"Yes!" Pandora appeared astounded that I was catching on so fast. I was shocked myself, but like I said, it wasn't exactly a surprise that there were paranormal happenings in Mystic Notch.

"I thought I saw images in there," I said.

"Thank the great cat god Bastet for that. You might be helpful after all."

"Um. Thanks." Was she being sarcastic? I hadn't thought of her that way before. Sarcasm didn't translate well through meows. "Last night, were you trying to show me something in the paperweight?"

"Right again!" Pandora stopped grooming. "There's something going on in Mystic Notch, and we need your help. I thought you might be able to see a clue in the paperweight.”

“Something bad?” That explained why I’d felt an ominous impending doom lately.

“Very bad, and us cats are trying to make sure that evil foes don’t harm our town.”

“Evil foes? Like who?” I was a tad skeptical because now this was starting to sound like an episode from a superhero movie.

“Felicity Bates, for one.”

I wasn’t so skeptical about that. I knew she was bad news.

Pandora continued. “And Sarah Delaney.”

“Oh no! I thought I saw Sarah running away from the shop earlier.”

“Yeah, that’s why I went the extra mile to try to talk to you. We need your help to—”

“Yoo-hoo, anyone here?”

I shushed Pandora, then spun around and looked out into the hall. Someone had come in, and I did not want them to hear me talking to my cat.

“I’ll be right out!”

“But I need to—”

“Shush! Later!” I interrupted Pandora and hurried out front.

Josie Martin was standing in the shop, looking down the hallway. She had a camera in one hand and a notebook in the other. “How are you, Willa?”

“Fine, you?” I was a bit distracted by Pandora,

who kept looking like she would open her mouth and start talking. I supposed that wouldn't be a problem if Josie couldn't hear her, but what if I slipped up and answered back? That wouldn't do at all. Thankfully, Pandora must have sensed my fears and remained silent.

"I'm good. I don't know if you've heard, but I'm doing features on the various shops in town and was hoping to get some photos and do a write-up on Last Chance Books."

"Oh. That's nice. I am kind of busy now, though." If you considered trying to talk to your cat about saving the town from evil busy.

"It will only take a few seconds. I need to get it in before the deadline. It will be printed on Friday. Very good for business."

"Okay, fine." Josie was persistent, and I knew she'd probably bug me until I agreed, so I figured I might as well let her do her thing. Besides, I needed some time to process this new development with Pandora. What exactly did the cat think I could do to help, and did I even want to do it?

PANDORA CURLED UP IN HER CAT BED ON THE windowsill while Willa answered a barrage of questions from Josie. Josie used an old-fashioned camera that she proceeded to make a show of taking photos with, including one of Pandora in her bed. Pandora preened and plumped out her tail for the photo.

Willa kept shooting warning glances at Pandora, so she eventually tuned them out. She got it. It was disturbing to realize you could talk to your cat, and Willa was worried Josie might find out and think it was strange.

Pandora shut her eyes, feeling quite pleased with herself. Wait until the barn cats found out she'd finally communicated with her human! If only Willa hadn't shushed her right before she told her the most important part. But the key was safe in the box on the shelf, and Pandora deserved a little cat nap. She could fill Willa in and have her take the key to Elspeth later.

Josie's incessant questions kept her from falling asleep.

"Did you inherit all the books in the shop from your grandmother?"

"How do you get new inventory?"

"What types of books are most popular?"

On and on. Even Willa must have gotten tired of it, as she eventually stopped following Josie and plopped down on the purple sofa.

Mercifully, Pandora was blessed with sleep, finally, and she didn't awaken until Josie was opening the door to leave.

"Well, thanks for letting me do this piece. It will be in Friday's paper. Toodles!"

"You're welcome!" Willa yawned from the sofa

then peeked around the store. "We need to continue our talk, and I need a coffee."

She got up and went to the little kitchenette in the back, and Pandora followed.

"Listen, there's something very important you have to do." Pandora knew it was a lot for Willa to process. It would be nice to ease her into this whole business with the book and the key, but Pandora didn't have time.

Willa's left brow ticked up as she sipped the coffee. "Seriously? Is this how it's going to be? You bossing me around? I think I liked it better when all that came out of your mouth were annoying meows."

Annoying meows? Pandora always thought her meows were sweet and endearing. "Just this once, but after that, we'll take turns bossing each other around if you want. Remember how I mentioned that the cats are here to protect Mystic Notch from evil-doers?"

"Yeah." Willa still looked a little skeptical.

"You can do something to help us right now. That recipe book you got wasn't a recipe book."

Willa's eyes narrowed. "You don't say? I thought it was kind of unusual, and there was so much interest."

"Yeah, and there's a reason for it. Come on, I'll show you." Pandora trotted out of the back room to the front, skidding to a stop and almost being trampled by Willa when she saw what was sniffing around near the sofa. Fluff on his pink leash, and on the other end of that leash, Felicity Bates.

"Hello, Willa. Did I hear you talking to someone?" Felicity was seated on the sofa as if she'd been lounging there all day. She raised her left brow and leaned over as if to see if someone would follow Willa out of the back room. Felicity had dark circles under her eyes, and her hair was a mess. Pandora hoped it wasn't because she was up all night trying to locate the key.

Willa stood there for a few seconds just staring at Felicity, who stared back with a smug smile on her face.

Fluff arched his back, puffed out his long white fur, and hissed.

Pandora did the same.

"Uhhh… I was just talking to myself." Willa glanced at Pandora uneasily. "Have you been here long?"

"Just a few minutes. This sofa is always so inviting. When I didn't see you in the shop, I figured I'd take a seat." Felicity stood, smoothed out the folds of her long white skirt, and tossed a lock of witchy red hair behind her shoulder.

Pandora glanced at the bells over the door. Had they been so engrossed in their conversation that they hadn't heard them ring? Had Felicity heard what she and Willa were talking about? She wouldn't put it past her to eavesdrop.

Pandora glared at Fluff while Willa went behind the counter. He looked as smug as his owner, as if they knew something Pandora and Willa didn't. Ha! The joke was on them if they were looking for the key. Pandora gave Fluff a sly smile and then turned abruptly, showing him her back end as she trotted behind the counter with her tail held high.

"So, what brings you here? I'm sure this isn't a social call." Willa crossed her arms over her chest as Felicity approached the counter with a book.

"I'd like to buy this book on smoothies. I also heard you have a very interesting cookbook here, and I'm in the mood to improve on my culinary skills."

Pandora snorted. Ha! She was a day late and a dollar short.

Willa shot Pandora a warning glance. Oops. Had she meowed that out loud? Luckily, the lines of communication between Felicity and Pandora were nonexistent. Unfortunately, the lines of communication between Fluff and Pandora were functioning just fine.

"Don't talk to my mistress that way," Fluff hissed in his presumptuous, snotty voice.

"I'll talk any way I see fit," Pandora replied.

Willa gave her a confused look. Willa probably couldn't hear Fluff and wondered why Pandora had randomly blurted that out. Pandora envied Willa. She wished that she couldn't hear Fluff either.

"Is it an old leather book that looks like it belongs

in a moldy castle with type-font that gets a little blurry?" Willa asked.

Felicity looked excited. "Yes!"

"Sorry, someone already bought that."

Felicity scowled. "What do you mean someone bought it? Who?"

"Mary Ashford picked it up about an hour ago." Willa gave Felicity a sorry-not-sorry look.

Felicity looked steamed. "You sold it to someone else? But I put my name on the list!"

Interesting choice of words. Pandora wondered why Willa would even add Felicity's name to the list. What if Felicity was speaking literally? She did claim to be a witch. Could she have used a writing charm or something to add her name?

If Felicity was looking for the cookbook, that meant she was looking for the key. Pandora glanced up at the shelf. Thankfully the box was still there.

But if Felicity was looking, then Pandora needed to get Willa on this right away. She couldn't wait for Felicity to leave.

"I'm sorry, Mary's name was *first* on the list, so I called her first, and she was interested, so I sold it to her."

Felicity narrowed her eyes at Willa. "Fine, then I'll just take this one." She slapped the book on the counter, and Willa rang her up. When Willa was done, she grabbed the bag and stormed out of the store, tugging Fluff behind her. Fluff turned to give Pandora one last hiss as the door closed in his face.

"The joke's on you. The key wasn't even in that book!" Pandora meowed, but not loud enough for them to hear. No sense in tipping them off to the fact that Willa had the key.

Pandora didn't waste any time. She turned to Willa. "This is of the utmost importance. I think Felicity was looking for a key. I was trying to tell you about it when we were interrupted. The key is very important. It was in the binding of that cookbook. It's magical, and you're gonna have to trust me on this, but if it falls into the wrong hands, you're not going to like what happens to Mystic Notch."

Willa looked skeptical, but then she seemed to give it careful consideration. Truth be told, Willa was a little slow on the uptake. The evidence that there was magic in Mystic Notch was all over the place, and Pepper had been trying to get her on board with it for a long time. Willa herself had seen evidence but didn't believe her own eyes. Hopefully, that was about to change. When you can see ghosts and talk to cats, how can you deny the existence of magic?

"Well, Felicity would certainly be the wrong hands, but where is the key, and what can I do about it?"

"Remember the key you found when you caught me with the recipe book on the floor?"

"Yes! Of course. You knew the key was in there? That's why you knocked the book over?"

"Well, not exactly. Actually, Franklin and Robert were fighting over it, and the key fell out. I was just trying to rescue it. But I did know it was magical."

"Wait, what do Franklin and Robert have to do with this?"

"Nothing, as far as I know. They were fighting over who might have recipes named after them or some such thing. You know how they are."

"That explains why you've been staring at that shelf." Willa walked over to the shelf where the box was. "What were you going to do with it?"

"I was going to take it to the cats to see that it got to Elspeth, and now that you know how important it is, I could use your help with that."

"Of course."

Relief washed over Pandora as Willa stretched to retrieve the box from the top shelf. She turned around, placing it on the counter, and Pandora jumped up to get a look inside. Pandora held her breath, her tail swishing back and forth eagerly as Willa undid the latch and—

The door to the shop burst open, the bells ringing wildly as if a tornado had burst into the room. It wasn't an actual tornado, but it was pretty close. Willa's sister, Gus, the county sheriff, stormed toward the counter, fury in her amber eyes. She wasn't a big person, but with her blond hair in a tight bun, her hat atop her head, and the look on her face, she seemed pretty big.

She slapped something on the counter and glared at Willa.

"Okay, Willa." Gus tapped the card she put on the counter. "Explain why Mystic Notch's latest murder victim had a meeting with you shortly before her death."

CHAPTER NINE

My gaze flicked from the box to my sister. I couldn't open it in front of her. She didn't understand about magic.

This was all a bit much to take. First, I find out that I can have a conversation with my cat, then she tells me there's a magical key in a box on my shelf that could harm the town, and now my sister is accusing me of being involved in a murder.

Gus was standing in front of me, brows raised, hands on hips, demanding an answer. I knew she wasn't really accusing me, and I couldn't blame her for storming in. When it came to investigations, I did get a little overzealous sometimes, and we'd had a few run-ins before. It wouldn't be accurate to say we didn't get along. Aside from murder investigations, we got along just great.

I glanced down at the card to see the familiar open book logo and the gold-embossed Last Chance Books lettering. Scribbled in pen was yesterday's date.

"Did you say someone was dead?" Willa felt terrible that someone had died. "Who?"

"Mary Ashford."

"Meow!" Pandora practically fell off the counter. I couldn't blame her. It didn't take someone who could speak cat to know that her meow translated to "Oh crap!" I felt the same way. The key had been in the recipe book, Mary had purchased the recipe book, and now Mary was dead.

"Oh, no. Mary did come here. She bought a recipe book." I picked up the card. "She came in yesterday. She'd been on a list in case an old recipe book came in, and I had called her."

Gus narrowed her eyes. "Did she seem nervous? Did you notice anything amiss? Anyone following her?"

It was just like Gus to interrogate me as if I were a suspect. I was used to it though, so the interrogation didn't faze me. The fact that Mary was dead, however, did. Pandora, too, if the way she was staring at the box was any indication.

"What was in the book?" Gus asked.

"Just recipes. Do you think something about the book is related to her death?"

Gus narrowed her eyes at me again. "Now, don't

go getting any ideas about investigating. The book probably isn't related. No one kills over a book, right?"

"Right." If she only knew.

"But somehow you always seem to be in the center of things."

"Not this time," I lied. If Mary was killed because of the book, then I was indeed in the center of things. I could point her in the right direction, though, and maybe if the killer was the person after the key as Pandora said, Gus could arrest them and put them in jail where they couldn't do any harm. "There is one thing, though."

"What?"

"Danielle Norden and Felicity Bates were both pretty upset that I sold the book to Mary."

Gus frowned. "Was it valuable?"

"No, I only charged twenty dollars."

Gus snorted. "You book people are real drama queens. Imagine Danielle and Felicity being mad over a twenty-dollar book. If you hear anything—and I know what a busybody you are, so I figure you prob-ably will—let me know."

She grabbed the business card and left.

"This does not bode well." Pandora said after the door closed and we were alone. "We need to get that key to Elspeth ASAP."

"You can say that again. I'll put it in the zipper

pocket of my purse and run it right over." I opened the lid of the box, and we both looked inside.

My stomach plummeted. The box was empty.

andora almost coughed up a hairball at the sight of the empty box. "Where is it? Did you move it?"

"No, I didn't move it." Willa's voice had a sarcastic tinge.

"What? It's not that outrageous of a question. It's only you and me here, and I certainly couldn't reach it up there. If I could, the key would already be safe with Elspeth. You're the only one that can reach it."

"Not the *only* one."

They both glanced toward the couch where Felicity had been only moments ago.

"You don't think that she could have taken it, do you? She was on the couch," Willa said. "We were only in the back room for a few minutes. I don't think she would have had time to get behind the counter, grab the box, take the key, and then plop onto the couch. How would she even know where the key was?"

Pandora trotted over to the couch and started sniffing around. It smelled like mothballs and mildew. How odd. She followed it to the counter, but there it faded away. "Maybe she used witchcraft."

"Maybe. But then why did she stay? Why ask about the recipe book and buy a book on smoothies, of all things?"

Pandora hopped back onto the counter and peered in the box again as if the key might magically appear. It didn't.

"It has to be Felicity. She's witchy enough to want to return to the scene of the crime and rub it in our faces." Willa picked up the box and turned it upside down and shook. Still no key, just a piece of black plastic.

Pandora batted at it with her paw. "This is not good. Not good at all." She punctuated the last word by drawing her paw back and batting the plastic off the counter.

"Maybe she had her evil cat jump up and get it." Pandora looked at the shelf. "Though I'm not sure that's possible without knocking things over."

"Felicity didn't act like she knew about the key, but I wouldn't put it past her to put on an act. She did seem a little off." Willa tapped her top lip with her finger. "There were other people that were interested too. Like Danielle. And she seemed very upset that I had sold the book to Mary."

Good point. Pandora reminded herself not to get tunnel vision about Felicity and Fluff. "And didn't you say Sarah Delaney was lurking around when you got back from your optometrist appointment?" Pandora glanced outside as if expecting to see the menacing antique dealer lurking on the sidewalk. "She's kind of shady, and we know she knows about magic."

"We do?"

"Yeah, it's obvious, don't you think?"

"She does dress like a witch."

"Let's not forget that the culprit might not be someone who looks like a witch. Most people actually try to hide the fact that they are magic, especially if they are up to no good," Pandora said.

"Good point. Let's approach this like an investigation. Back at my old job…" Willa launched into a diatribe on the proper steps to take in order to conduct an investigation.

Pandora started cleaning behind her ears. Willa used to be a crime journalist years ago, and she could get a little long-winded when she started going over what steps she saw fit to take during an investigation. Usually, she was just talking out loud to herself, and no matter how many complaining meows Pandora made, she did not stop. This time, Pandora supposed she could tell her to stop, but she didn't want to be rude. Best to just focus on her daily grooming and let Willa get it out.

"So, let's figure out who had opportunity." Willa got the broom out, presumably to sweep up the plastic Pandora had batted off the counter. "I put the key in the box two days ago. Since then, we've had several customers, but I don't think any of them have been behind the counter."

"Sarah Delaney was near, but I don't think she came in. I would have noticed," Pandora said. At least, she hoped she would have, but what if Sarah put a sleep spell on her or something?

"Felicity was here. Josie was here taking photographs, but we were watching her the whole time."

Pandora's tail twitched. Maybe Willa had been watching her the whole time, but Pandora had been sleeping. Still, what would Josie want with the key, and how would she even know it was there? How would any of them? Pandora didn't know who was a witch and who wasn't. There were plenty of magical people in Mystic Notch who hid their true identities, so no one could be ruled out.

"And Gus." Pandora snorted. They both knew Gus was the most non-magical person in the Notch.

Willa laughed as she bent down with the dustpan. "Then there's Mary and Danielle. Danielle was mad about the book and knew Mary had it. If one of them thought the key was in the book, they would have discovered that it wasn't, and where is the most logical place for them to look?"

"Here."

"Is the key so important that someone would kill for it?" Willa dumped the contents of the dustpan into the trash.

"It is." Pandora's spirits sank even more. Did a villain have the key? And what would they use it for? Did it really open a portal that could unleash horrible creatures and dark magic?

"Let's look on the bright side. Maybe Gus will figure out who killed Mary, and that will solve our problem. That person will be put in jail and won't be able to do anything with the key," Willa said.

"I wish it were that easy. Unfortunately, I have a sneaking suspicion that several people are looking for the key," Pandora said. "If only we had surveillance in the shop, we could see who came in."

"I think it's a good thing that the crime rate is so low it's not warranted." Willa tapped the box with her fingernail and scanned the shop. "But we might have something just as good."

Pandora cocked her head at her human.

"Robert and Franklin. If they were hanging around, they might have seen something."

"Good idea!" Maybe teaming up with Willa

wasn't going to be so bad. Pandora looked around, her eyes searching for a whisper of ghostly vapor, her nose sniffing for a hint of ectoplasmic goo, her ears straining to hear a ghostly wail. Nothing. "Too bad they don't always appear when you want them to."

"No, but I know how to summon them." Willa took off toward the historical section of the store. Pandora jumped down from the counter and trotted after her.

Willa went straight for a biography of Franklin Pierce and pulled it out of the stacks. It was an old tome, almost four inches thick and a little dusty on the top.

"This is the thickest Franklin Pierce biography I have," she yelled into the store, making Pandora jump and wish she could cover her ears. "I hope I don't drop it!"

Willa held the book in the palm of her hand, tilting her hand toward the floor. The book started to slide.

Whoosh!

Pandora heard the ghostly sound and felt the chill just before Franklin Pierce appeared wearing a topcoat and tails, his hand outstretched below the book as if to catch it before it fell to the floor.

"Whoa, now, Willa, you don't want to damage that book!" Franklin looked appalled at the thought.

"Why not? It's bloated up with fluff. Look how

thick it is." Robert Frost had appeared beside Franklin. He was dressed in a tweed suit with a bow tie. "You'll never see any of the books on me padded like that."

Franklin frowned at Robert. "There is a lot more to be said about me. I was the president of the United States, in case you've forgotten."

"I brought joy to many with my exquisite poetry!" Robert retorted.

"No fighting, guys." Willa slid the book back into its spot on the shelf. "I have an important question."

"Is it about how to rhyme a certain word? I'm very good at that," Robert said.

"That's child's play." Franklin turned to Willa. "Perhaps our favorite shop owner needs a lesson in foreign policy."

"Those are both worthy questions," Willa said. "But it's neither. I was wondering whether either of you happened to see anyone in here take something from the shelf behind the counter."

Their ghostly gazes turned toward the front of the store.

"I don't think so. What is it that you think they took?"

"The key that fell out of the recipe book when you guys were fighting over it," Pandora cut in.

"Oh that! Yes, I do remember that key," Robert said. "I think it used to be mine. You see, the distinctive shape with the notch on the top reminds me of one that opened my writing box."

"Really?" Willa looked interested, but Pandora rolled her eyes. Now she'd have to suffer through some story about his beloved writing box that held his best-selling poems.

Robert got all misty-eyed. "It was a lovely box about this size." Robert mimed the size of a bread box. "It was tiger maple inlaid with ivory on the edges and a thin gold strip."

Franklin, not to be outdone, said, "I had a decanter box just like that except it also had my initials on it."

Robert gave him a look and cleared his throat. "Yes, but mine was special. I had never sold a poem until I started keeping my work in that box. Suddenly my work became very popular."

"That's nice, but you don't think it was really the box, do you?" Willa glanced at Pandora. She seemed skeptical, but now that she was getting on board with magic, maybe not so much.

Robert laughed. "Probably not. It's just my old superstition bubbling up. But I do miss that box. Of course, my sister and my friend, Joshua Duggins, wouldn't miss it."

"Why not?"

"They used to joke it was cursed. When they each opened it, something bad happened."

"Like what?"

"Well, my sister fell off her horse that very after-noon and broke her arm, and Joshua lost his job. Not to mention, it rained for ten days straight after he opened it."

"Could have been coincidence," Franklin said.

"What about when you opened it? Sounds like it was good luck for you," Pandora said.

"Yes, it was! Nothing but sunshine and roses when I opened it. Everyone used to joke that it was cursed, and I was the only one who could open it without the evil getting out." Robert stroked his chin. "I should write a poem about that. Anyway, that's why I always kept it locked. Didn't want anyone to get bad luck."

"Or to see your poems and possibly steal them," Franklin said.

"That too."

Robert made sense. The cats had been worried the key opened a portal. Pandora had been picturing some sort of a door, but maybe the portal was Robert's writing box. Where was that box now? Hopefully not with the person that had taken the key. If it wasn't, they still had a chance.

"I didn't see a thing, but I've been out at some ghostly baking contests trying to see if anyone is cooking up a batch of Robert Frosted Lemon Drops or Path Less Traveled Fudge." Robert looked at Franklin. "What about you?"

"I've been busy too. Looking for the origins of the Franklin Pierced Frankfurters recipe." Franklin looked at Willa. "Sorry, but we just aren't in the store at all times."

Willa looked as disappointed as Pandora felt. "Are you sure? You saw no one behind the counter? What about Felicity Bates? Or Sarah Delaney?"

The ghosts shrugged. "Sorry."

"Darn."

Willa blew out a breath. "Looks like we're going to have to investigate this the old-fashioned way. I think we should look into Felicity Bates first."

"At least now we may have two items to look for. If that key really was Robert's, we can look for the box and the key. Hopefully we can keep them from ending up in the same hands."

Willa pulled out her phone. "I'll message Striker and see if he wants to get together for dinner. Hopefully, I can get some information out of him about the murder investigation. That's got to be connected, don't you think?"

Pandora puffed out with pride that Willa was asking her opinion. Of course, she knew that she, as the cat, was the superior being, but she wasn't sure Willa had realized that. She couldn't wait to report to the Mystic Notch cats that she'd communicated with her human and that human knew who the boss was. But her euphoric feeling of excitement was short-lived because she would also have to tell them that they lost the key.

"I guess I'll need to report back to the cats and

see what they say. First… can I have some of those salmon cat treats you hide in the filing cabinet?" There were going to be advantages to being able to talk to Willa, not the least of which was requesting exactly what Pandora wanted for dinner.

CHAPTER ELEVEN

I checked my messages when I got in the car. There was a reply from Steve Wheeler about the bathroom remodel. When I'd contacted him before, I'd assumed the tea was for me to drink because Pepper sensed that I wasn't getting the hint from Striker. But then Pandora drank it, and now we could communicate. Maybe I'd been wrong, and it had nothing to do with Striker wanting to take things to the next level and me not noticing.

I glanced over at Pandora.

"What?" Pandora seemed annoyed.

"You drank Pepper's tea, and then we could talk to each other. Do you think the tea did that?"

"Duh." Pandora looked at her like she was stupid. "Why do you think I drank that vile concoction in the first place?"

I didn't know what to say. I didn't want to admit

to my cat that I thought the tea was because Striker wanted more out of our relationship. So, did that mean I shouldn't have the bathroom redone?

"Striker's coming for dinner. I'm going to see what I can get out of him about the investigation."

"See if they found any white cat hairs at the scene," Pandora said just before curling into a ball. "I'm going to take a snooze. I have a lot to discuss at Elspeth's barn, and I need to be on my game."

I drove the rest of the way in silence, listening to Pandora's little snores. I wished I could fall asleep as fast as she could. When I pulled into the driveway of my white Victorian house, she stirred.

"We're here already?" She stretched and waited for me to open the door then jumped out and started toward the woods.

"Hey, where are you going?" I called after her.

"To Elspeth's barn," Pandora shot over her shoulder.

"You go there by yourself?"

Pandora stopped and turned around, cocking her head to the side, her tail swishing high in the air with the hooked end pointing toward the woods. "I do a lot of things by myself that you don't know about. Just because we can communicate now doesn't mean you can boss me around."

"Okay, right."

Pandora trotted off, and I turned toward the farmer's porch next to the driveway that I used as an entrance, muttering under my breath. "Just see if you get the salmon-flavor food again."

IN THE KITCHEN, I PULLED OUT SOME PLATES AND SET the kitchen table. *Should I put a candle in the middle?* No, that was getting too romantic. But maybe some romance would help get information about the case out of Striker. Before I could decide, his car was pulling in. He hopped out with a paper bag and let himself in the side door. It felt good that he was comfortable enough to just walk in. I thought again about the toothbrush holder.

"I got subs this time. I'm kind of pizza'd out," Striker said.

"Did you get my favorite?" I loved roast beef with extra pickles and lots of mayonnaise.

Striker grinned and kissed me on the lips. "You bet I did."

We unpacked the subs and sat down at the table. Striker frowned, looking around the kitchen. "Where is Pandora?"

What should I say? I couldn't exactly say the cat had told me she was going to Elspeth's. Striker knew that I didn't let Pandora out on her own. Truth be told, I was a little worried. The woods could be dangerous, and I was afraid a coyote or other animal might get Pandora. Though, judging by the way she had confidently stalked off, she'd done this before.

And now that we could actually talk to each other, I didn't feel like I could tell Pandora not to go to the barn alone. It was clear that Pandora did not want to be bossed around, and I had a sneaking suspicion that continuing to do so might not bode well for me.

"Last I saw, she was lying down in the living room. She might be a little under the weather today. She's been a bit sleepy." I figured that would explain why she wasn't in the kitchen looking for a food hand-out. I wasn't ready to tell Striker I could talk to my cat. Even though we'd shared the fact that we could both see ghosts, talking cats was a whole different story.

"I hope she's okay." Striker bit into a steak-and-cheese sub and made *yum yum* noises.

I picked a pickle out of my sub. "I'm sure she's fine. Gus came by accusing me of being involved with Mary Ashford's murder."

Striker chuckled. "Good to see Gus is back to her old self. But of course, you're not a suspect."

"I know. Mary came in and bought a book from me. That's why she had my card."

"That's what Gus said." Striker continued to focus on his sub. Obviously he wasn't going to offer up any more information. I'd have to ask outright.

"So, how is that investigation going? Any leads?" Then I hastened to add, "I only ask because Danielle

Norden had been very upset that Mary got the book, and I was afraid I had offered her as a suspect in Gus's mind."

"Gus did have her as a suspect. But we've already interviewed her, and she has an alibi. So don't worry, you didn't get her into trouble."

Good. I took a bite of my sub. It was delicious with crusty bread, tangy horseradish, pickles, and creamy mayonnaise, which all blended in perfectly with the rare roast beef.

"It's scary that Mary was killed that way." I was fishing because I had no idea how she was killed.

"You mean bludgeoned?"

"Yeah, gross." So, she wasn't killed magically, apparently. Bludgeoning seemed like a good old-fashioned non-magical homicide method.

"Anything interesting at the scene, like maybe white cat hairs?"

Striker stopped chewing and looked at me suspiciously. Maybe I'd gone too far with that question. "Cat hairs? You mean like in the last case?"

"Yeah, exactly." Fluff had been at the center of the other case.

"Nothing like that." Striker continued to munch on his sub.

"Do you have any leads?" I tried to sound like I was just making idle conversation.

"We're tracking a few things down. Mary lived alone on an isolated road with one other neighbor, and the neighbor didn't see anything unusual. But don't worry, we'll find out who did it," Striker said.

"I have the utmost confidence that you will." I did, but that didn't help me much with my own investigation. I had no idea if Mary's killer was looking for the key. Maybe it was an old boyfriend or disgruntled coworker. But I did know something that police didn't. If the killer was looking for the key, then the murder might have magical connotations. Maybe Gus and Striker hadn't asked exactly the right questions of Mary's neighbor.

I eased off on the questioning, and the conversation turned to more mundane topics. As we ate, I couldn't keep my thoughts from wandering to how Pandora was making out with the Mystic Notch cats in Elspeth's barn.

PANDORA'S WHISKERS TWITCHED WITH EXCITEMENT AS she slipped through the opening in Elspeth's barn door.

The cats were in their usual positions. Some were busy eating at the stainless steel dishes. Some were napping in the beds Elspeth had lined up in the back. Others were grooming themselves atop the many bales of hay.

"Big news!" Pandora called out. "I have finally communicated with my human."

"Meow?" Otis looked down from his position in the loft. His mouth was opening but only meow sounds were coming out. What was up with that?

Maybe Otis was playing a joke on her. She turned to see Inkspot passing through the sliver of moonlight as he made his way from the back of the barn.

"Greetings, Inkspot. I have good news and bad news." Pandora bowed slightly in deference to Inkspot's standing as their leader.

"Meow." Inkspot's deep baritone was unmistakable, but why was she only hearing meows and not words?

Pandora looked around in a panic. The other cats were now trotting up. Sasha, Kelley, Hope. All their mouths were moving, but all she could hear was a cacophony of mews and meows.

They were looking at her funny too. Their heads tilted, their eyes questioning, their tails twitching.

"Can't you guys understand me? What is going on? I drank the tea, and now I can talk to Willa." Oh no. She drank the tea. Pepper's teas were known to backfire.

The panic grew stronger.

She tried again. "Maybe this is just temporary. You guys can hear me now, right? We have an issue. The key is missing from the box, and we don't know who took it. I need your help!"

The cats looked at each other in confusion.

"Meero?"

"Merow?"

"Merep?"

It was no use. She couldn't understand them, and judging by the confused looks on their faces, they couldn't understand her either.

Pandora hung her head and turned to leave the barn. Without the wisdom and help of the cats, how were they ever going to find the key?

CHAPTER TWELVE

The next morning, I shuffled downstairs in my pajamas at six thirty. Striker had left to go back to his place the night before, stating that he had to get to work early. Had he left because of the tiny bathrooms? I made a mental note to reply to Steve. I wasn't sure if I would spring for a remodel now unless I got some hint from Striker. Maybe just a double toothbrush holder would do.

I hadn't seen Pandora the night before and was a bit anxious to find out if she made it home okay. A quick peek in the kitchen showed that she'd eaten the treats I'd put in her bowl. She was safe.

I had a half hour before I had to leave for work, so I shuffled into the living room with a cup of coffee. The paperweight on the coffee table tugged at my attention. I sat on the couch and lifted it up, gazing into it.

I held it in front of my face. Would I see a clue in there? But all I saw was an upside-down image of the other side of the room. I tilted it this way and that, but it still looked like my living room, although a little fuzzy.

Where had I put my reading glasses? It was hard getting used to them, and I kept leaving them places, but maybe they would help me hone in on something inside the glass orb.

I found them between the couch cushions. After sliding them on, I lay down and held the paperweight up over my face, but once again, I saw only the ceiling and a black dot, which I thought was a bug on the other side of the glass orb at first.

"What are you lying around for? We have a problem." I turned my head to see Pandora sitting on the floor, frowning up at me.

"Sorry, I was looking to see if I could find a clue in the paperweight." I sat back up and put it on the table. Pandora looked all blurry, and it made me disoriented for a minute until I realized I still had my reading glasses on. "You did say this was like a crystal ball, right?"

Pandora hopped up on the table and peered into the paperweight. "Yeah. You didn't see anything?"

"Just an upside-down image of the room."

Pandora pushed the paperweight aside. "We've got bigger fish to fry. It turns out Pepper's tea had some unexpected consequences."

I frowned. Of course it did. Her teas always had some unintended consequences. "What?"

"It turns out I can no longer talk to Elspeth's cats." Pandora looked so dejected that I felt sorry for her. I reached out my hand to pet her fur.

"Is that really bad?" I asked.

Pandora rolled her eyes. "Yeah. Without being able to communicate with them, we can't coordinate our efforts. Normally, we would branch out around town and spy on people. I was planning on having them spy on Sarah Delaney and Felicity to see if they did anything strange. But now I have no idea what they are doing, and they have no idea what we are doing. We're practically on our own."

"I bet we can figure this out on our own," I said, hoping I wasn't being naively optimistic. "We already have some pretty strong clues that it was Felicity, right?"

"Right. What did you find out from Striker?"

"Not much. Danielle is in the clear because she had an alibi. The neighbors saw and heard nothing. Mary lived on a remote road with just one neighbor, but I was thinking they might've asked the questions for normal murder, and this is a paranormal murder. Maybe we should talk to the neighbor and ask different types of questions."

"Good thinking." Pandora's approval made me flush with pride.

"Did you find out how she was murdered?"

"Bludgeoned."

Pandora shivered. "Time of day?"

"I didn't get that. I have to pick and choose my questions because if I ask too much, he gets suspicious. You know how Striker is. He doesn't want to give out police information."

"You need to be sneakier to get anything out of him, but at least he's easier than Gus."

We exchanged an eye roll. Both of us knew Gus wouldn't let out even a syllable of information on a case.

"It could also be that Mary's murder had nothing to do with magic. Maybe she really did just want an old recipe book. She has a food blog, and she said she was doing a feature on old recipes," I said.

"It could be. But we need to research all angles," Pandora said. "And we also need to talk to Pepper. That tea messed up communication with the other cats. Hopefully, she can fix that." Pandora looked me up and down. "Are you going to lounge around all day in your pajamas? Get a move on. It's time to go to work. And could you throw some of those chicken-flavored treats in your bag for later? I feel a craving coming on."

THE REGULARS WERE WAITING AT THE DOOR WHEN Pandora and I arrived a half hour later.

"Morning, Willa. How are things with you today?" Bing handed me a coffee. I sensed his words might have a hidden meaning, and I glanced at Pandora. Bing and Elspeth were good friends, and he'd been a magician. Could it be that he was magic too? I didn't want to ask him in front of everyone else, so I simply said, "Great, and you?"

"Just fine."

I opened the door, and everyone got settled in their places on the sofa and chairs.

"I suppose you've heard the news from your sister and young man," Hattie said.

I nodded, assuming that she was referring to the murder.

"Seems to be happening all too often here in Mystic Notch." Cordelia shook her head.

"You mean the murder?" Josiah asked. Apparently, he wasn't as perceptive as I was.

"Yes. Poor Mary." Hattie glanced at me. "Do you know any of the details?"

"You know Gus and Striker never tell me the details of the case," I said. "But Mary was in here looking for a recipe book that day."

Bing's bushy white brows slid up. "What kind of a recipe book?"

"A very old one. In fact, the same book that Felicity Bates was looking for."

He leaned forward. "And did Felicity know that Mary had the book?"

"Yes, she did."

"A recipe book?" Hattie turned to Cordelia. "Wasn't Felicity arguing with that Sarah Delaney about recipes at the Cut & Curl?"

"She was. How odd." Cordelia looked at me. "But surely recipes had nothing to do with murder."

"Yeah, that would be silly," I said. But I thought the exact opposite. If the two seniors could remember more about the argument, that might be useful information. Pandora must have been thinking the same thing because she was sitting beside my chair, watching the two sisters intently. "What else did they say?"

"I don't remember much. Just something about the spices, like I said before," Cordelia said.

"Ask about the key," Pandora said. I glanced around to see if anyone had heard anything other than her usual meow, but apparently no one had.

"Did they mention anything about an old book or maybe a key?" I asked.

"A key? Let me think." Cordelia tilted her head and closed her eyes as if to visualize. "They were sitting at the nail table. Felicity was getting that bright-red color, and Sarah her usual black to match what she always wears. First, they were ignoring each other, and then they started sniping back and forth. They might've talked about keys, but I only remember the spices. What about you, Hattie?"

"I don't think they mentioned a key. The thing is,

I got very sleepy, and most of it is fuzzy. I have to admit, I might've dozed off. Why would they talk about a key?"

"Just wondering. Felicity was in here and mentioned something." I was intentionally vague so I didn't have to lie.

"Well, anyway, it's a shame about Mary. She told me her blog was just starting to take off," Cordelia said.

"I heard Josie Martin was doing a feature on it," Hattie added.

"Speaking of Josie Martin, I saw her here. Is she doing that article on the bookstore?" Josiah asked.

"Yes. She took all kinds of pictures and asked all kinds of questions. I guess it's supposed to be in Friday's paper."

Hattie patted her hair. "I hope you mentioned us. Maybe we should see if Josie wants a picture."

Had I mentioned them? I really couldn't remember. "Of course I mentioned you."

"Well, we need to get going. There's a sale down at the department store, and we need some new outfits." Hattie finished her tea, and the two sisters stood.

"Me too. I need to stop by the post office," Josiah said. "And looks like you've got some customers coming in."

The door opened, and two women came in,

smiling and laughing. They nodded at us and made their way into the bookshelves.

The regulars left, and Pandora and I got behind the counter. I had some work to catch up on.

Pandora got into her bed in the window. "Wake me when it's time to go visit Mary's neighbor."

Pandora was down in the dumps. She'd tried to nap for a few hours, but her loss of ability to communicate with the other cats had hit her hard. Striker hadn't revealed anything concrete, Franklin and Robert were no help as to who could have stolen the key, and the bookstore regulars' memories about the argument between Felicity and Sarah Delany were suspect. Things were not going well. Not well at all.

She glanced over at Willa, who was standing at the counter typing on her laptop. She had her new reading glasses on but was adjusting the angle of her head and squinting. Probably doing the infernal inventory that seemed to be never-ending with this business.

Why was she fiddling around with book inventory when they had a lead to talk to? Mary's neighbor might have seen or heard something that the police wouldn't take notice of. Maybe a ghostly sound or eerie lights. And Pandora wanted to inspect the scene of the crime. The police would have removed all the normal clues, but maybe she could find some paranormal ones.

"Why are you messing about with that? We need to find Mary's neighbor and start asking some questions." Pandora did her best downward dog stretch so she could be limber for the interrogation.

Willa's fingers stilled. She gritted her teeth and gave Pandora a forced smile. Uh-oh. Maybe she should have been less forceful. "For your information, I was just looking up Mary's address so I could search for who else lives on that street."

"Oh, yeah. That's smart." Pandora hoped her compliment would make up for the snarky remark.

"Mary lives—lived—on Maple, and I think that's where Jennifer Jones lives. Let me look in my customer database." Willa typed in a few strokes and hit return. "Yep. We're in luck. Jennifer is a good customer, and I know how we can get an excuse to talk to her."

"How?" Despite Pandora's impatience, she was impressed at Willa's sleuthing skills and grateful that she'd taken her warning about the key to heart.

"I'll show you." A few mouse clicks later, the printer whirred to life. Willa pulled the paper off and held up a giant fifty-percent-off coupon. "I'm going to personally deliver a coupon to her in appreciation for her patronage. Not too many people are going to question fifty percent off."

"Good idea." Pandora hopped out of her bed and headed for the door. "Let's get a move on. There's no time to lose."

JENNIFER JONES WAS A MIDDLE-AGED BUSYBODY WHO lived in a small cape with a weed-strewn front yard. The curtains pulled across her living room window twitched as soon as I pulled in.

"Looks like Jennifer keeps a watch on the street. This might be our lucky break," Pandora said. She looked like she was ready to leap across me and out of the car as soon as I opened the door. Showing up at someone's front door with my pet cat felt awkward.

"I think you should stay here," I said.

"What, and miss all the fun?"

"It might put Jennifer off to see a cat standing beside me." I also didn't want to have to try to block out the incessant questions I knew Pandora would be trying to feed me.

"I'm not going to Jennifer's. I'm going to sniff around the crime scene." Pandora jerked her head down the street, where we could see another small house with yellow crime scene tape on the front door.

"Oh, right. Good idea."

I opened the door, and we both got out.

"Don't forget to ask about paranormal sights and sounds," she called over her shoulder as she trotted down the road. I was beginning to realize it was just like her to try to get the last bossy word in.

I made my way to Jennifer's peeling door and knocked.

After a few seconds, Jennifer answered, looking confused. "Willa Chance from the bookstore?"

"Hi, Jennifer." I thrust the coupon out. "I was just delivering some coupons for my best customers."

She took the coupon and looked at it with suspicion. "By hand? You couldn't just mail them?"

"I like to give the personal touch."

"Okay. Thanks." She stepped back as if she was going to close the door, and I had to think quick.

"I had one for Mary, too, but then I heard the awful news."

Her eyes flicked down the road toward Mary's house. "Yes, terrible thing. I hate to think of a killer loose on the street."

"Don't worry, my sister won't let that happen for long."

"I'm keeping my doors locked and shades drawn."

"Can't blame you. It's scary when it hits close to home. Were you here when it happened?"

Jennifer tugged her cardigan around her. "I believe so. Apparently, it happened in broad daylight.

Your sister asked me if I heard anything around three, and it gave me the willies because I was home at that time."

Aha! So, the time of death was three. I had learned something about the murder already. "Terrifying. I'm glad you didn't see or hear anything. That wouldn't be a memory you'd want."

"No indeed."

"But it's so quiet here. I'm surprised you didn't hear anything. I imagine you might have heard something even if maybe you didn't realize it was Mary."

Jennifer's eyes narrowed. "Did your sister send you here? That's pretty similar to what she asked me."

"Oh no, just wondering. Gus would never send me to ask questions. I was just thinking that if you saw some weird lights or heard a ghostly noise, that would be something that would haunt you." I actually had no idea what noises or sights one might see with a paranormal murder, but I supposed it would depend on the murder method. Since Mary had been bludgeoned, maybe there was nothing paranormal to be seen.

"Yeah. I guess it's a good thing there were no sounds." She glanced warily down the street. "Mary was a nice neighbor. Kept to herself. And I liked her blog. I made a few of her recipes from it, you know."

"Oh, really? She had just gotten a recipe book from my store."

"She was becoming more popular. Josie Martin was even here doing an article on her for the Gazette yesterday too. I saw her drive by."

"Such a shame she'll never see that."

"It is." Jennifer cast another glance down the street. "Well, thanks for the discount. I'll be in to the store soon."

I wracked my brain for a way to keep her talking just in case there was something more I could learn, but I didn't even know what to ask, and she closed the door pretty fast.

"You're welcome," I said to the closed door.

My phone pinged as I headed back to the car. It was Steve Wheeler, who was at my house waiting for me. *Darn it!* I'd been so busy with the realization I could talk to my cat and that the town was about to be ruined that I'd forgotten to cancel the appointment to look at my bathroom. Maybe we could swing by the house on the way to the shop. I got into the car and drove the short distance to Mary's to see if I could find Pandora. Hopefully, she'd had better luck than I did.

PANDORA TROTTED UNDER THE CRIME SCENE TAPE AND up to the house. She sniffed the front doorway then all around the foundation. She was looking for the smell of magic. Even though the murder had happened yesterday, the residual smell of magic should be here if Mary was killed paranormally.

She didn't smell magic out front, just fear, jealousy, and cinnamon muffins.

She made her way out back, detecting the faint aroma of freshly tilled earth and lavender with just the tiniest bit of burning hair. The scent of magic, and not the good kind either.

She didn't find any clues as to whose magic, though. If she could only get inside, she might find something, but the house was locked up tight. Maybe she could see something through one of the windows, but they were too high for her to see into.

She heard a rustle behind her and spun around, her blood freezing when she saw a fluffy white cat emerging from the woods at the edge of the property.

"What are you doing here?" Fluff asked.

"What are you?" she shot back. Wait, she could understand him? Maybe her inability to talk to cats had only been temporary. If that were true, then maybe she'd be able to hear the barn cats.

Please, for the love of Bastet, don't let it be that I can only hear Fluff.

"I asked first." Fluff ventured into the yard.

"I'm investigating the scene of the crime," Pandora said. "What are *you* doing here?"

"Same."

"Trying to make sure that there's no evidence incriminating your mistress?" Pandora asked.

"You think Felicity did this?" Fluff shook his head and started sniffing a rhododendron.

"She's the obvious suspect. Everyone knows she's a witch."

Fluff puffed out his tail in pride. "Really? Some question that, but while it's true, she's not looking for the key for the reasons you might think."

"You mean to wreak havoc on Mystic Notch? Those reasons?"

"Why would she want to do that? We live here. Her motivations might surprise you."

"No doubt." Pandora hissed.

Fluff sighed and hung his head. "I know Felicity has done some bad things, but this time it isn't about any of that."

"Like I would believe anything you say." Pandora turned her attention back to the house. If only she could get up to that window.

"This time you can."

Pandora whirled around. "Really? Aren't you the one that almost burned me and Hope to death in the shed? Hasn't your mistress been trying to wreak havoc in the town for years? And aren't you collecting the items on Hester Warren's list?" Pandora asked. "Come to think of it, where is that list?"

"We've only got part of it. But we weren't going to use items for anything bad. Felicity just wants to be in power. She is misunderstood." Fluff blinked, and

Pandora thought she saw a tear in his eye. "And so am I."

"I know this is one of your tricks, so you can stop the act."

"Sadly, it is not a trick. My mistress is desperate. She needs the key, or her time may be limited."

Something about the tremulous tone of Fluff's voice gave Pandora pause. She studied him with fresh eyes. His fur was dull, his whiskers droopy. And were those real tears coming out of his eyes?

No. She could not feel sympathetic toward him. This was just one of his tricks.

"You gave yourself away because you mentioned the key. How do you even know about that?" Pandora asked.

"We have our ways. We know what was in the recipe book, and Mary must have had it." Fluff narrowed his eyes. "That's why you're here, to see if the book and key are still here, isn't it?"

"Maybe." Pandora didn't need to tell him about the missing key. She knew better than to give away that vital information. "What evil do you plan to do with it?"

As Fluff stared at her, his whole being seemed to deflate. She sensed he was mulling over whether to tell her something, but was it a lie or the truth?

"We don't plan to do evil. My mistress needs the key to open the portal."

"Aha! So that's your plan, to let all kinds of demons and other undesirable creatures out."

"No, no!" Fluff shook his head violently. "She needs it because she has been the victim of a potion gone wrong."

Pandora could identify with that. "And what potion might that be?"

"Some sort of potion that humans like to make them more viable. That is why I am here without her. She is very ill." Fluff sniffed. "I fear she doesn't have much time left."

"So, you hope to find the key here?" Pandora had a sudden pang of sympathy for Fluff. She almost felt bad not cluing him in on the fact that the key wasn't here.

"I fear the key is no longer here. I was hoping to get a peek inside to determine who had done this. Assuming they succeeded in their mission to get the key from Mary, I will need to track them."

"I'm afraid you'll be disappointed. The place is locked up tighter than a drum."

Fluff eyed the window. "Maybe we don't need to actually go inside."

"The windows are too high."

"Maybe we can help each other." Fluff trotted over to the window, looking up at it. "The window is too high to jump to from the ground level, but if you are a little higher, perhaps you could look in."

"How would that happen?"

Fluff squared off under the window. "Get on my back, and perhaps you can jump up enough to hang on to the sill."

Pandora was skeptical. She'd been fooled by Fluff before, but how could it do any harm? She would be standing on *his* back, not the other way around. And she really, really wanted to see inside.

Bounding up onto him, she coiled her back legs and sprang off his back, unsheathing her front claws and reaching toward the windowsill. The sharp tips dug into the wood, her back claws grappling on the siding to boost herself up so she could look inside.

The house was a mess. She was a little dismayed at the way the police had left it. Maybe she'd have Willa talk to Gus or Striker about that. She could see a bloodstain on the carpet where Mary had fallen. There must have been a struggle, because things were knocked over. But the thing that shocked her the most was the old cookbook. It lay on the floor with all the pages ripped out and the binding torn. That proved it. Whoever had killed Mary had been looking for the key.

CHAPTER FOURTEEN

"Okay, I have a big surprise," Pandora said as I held the passenger-side door open so she could hop into the car.

"Did you find something?" I asked, hopeful that she had.

"Sort of. I ran into Fluff, and guess what?"

"What?" I didn't think anything good could come out of running into Fluff, but what did I know?

"I could talk to him. I could hear what he said. It makes me wonder if maybe the potion only lasted a little while."

I mulled that over. "I suppose it could be true. I know some of the potions Pepper has done before only lasted a little while. But you can still talk to me, so I wouldn't get my hopes up."

"Good point." Pandora looked a bit disappointed. "That's not all. I found something useful for the investigation too. But I really need to talk to the barn cats. Could we take a swing by before we go back to the shop?"

"I have to meet with Steve Wheeler at the house. Maybe you can take a quick trip to the barn while I talk to him."

"That sounds good."

Pandora stared out the window, apparently more concerned with seeing if she could communicate with Elspeth's cats than telling me what she discovered at the crime scene. "What else did you find out?"

"Huh? Oh yeah, sorry. According to Fluff, Felicity has some sort of an issue from a potion gone wrong. She's looking for the key, but not to wreak havoc on the Notch. She needs it to help with her issue."

"What sort of issue?"

"Something about making herself more viable. Fluff didn't really elaborate, but the point is he seemed very upset. I got the impression he was sincere. He even helped me look into Mary's window, and that's when I saw the recipe book."

"So, the killer didn't take the book, but they did look inside it. They must have known about the key," I said.

"And when they didn't find it in the book, they went to the last place the book was."

"The bookstore," I said. "But how did they know where to find it? And who took it? We know Felicity was there, but if she sent Fluff to Mary's, wouldn't that indicate that she isn't the one who took the key?"

Pandora's whiskers twitched. "That's a good question. Why would she send Fluff if she had the key already? Unless there is something else she needs to make the key work for her."

"Maybe it wasn't her. I admit, I'd like it if it was, but we shouldn't focus on her too much."

"True. Did you get any good leads from the neighbor?"

"Unfortunately, she didn't see or hear anything. I did find out the time of death though. Jennifer said that Gus asked her if she heard anything around three p.m. So, I assume that's when Mary was killed."

"No kidding. Well, I guess at least that's something."

PANDORA WAS FULL OF OPTIMISM AS SHE RACED through the woods to Elspeth's barn. Why Willa needed to meet with the carpenter to renovate the bathrooms was a mystery to Pandora, but it had worked out perfectly because now she could update the cats.

The barn door was open as usual, and she slipped inside. The barn looked different in daylight, and she could see most of the cats were there, dozing in the sun. As she entered, they picked up their heads, their ears perking up.

"Hey guys, I'm back! I don't know what happened before. I drank some weird tea from Pepper, but I think I'm back to normal now, and I have so much to tell you!"

"Meout?" Inkspot looked at her, concern in his green eyes.

"Merow?" Sasha came trotting over.

"Mew?" Otis looked at her with something that resembled pity. Pandora's heart sank.

"Come on, you guys. You're kidding right?" she asked hopefully.

"Meow meroo maroop." Hope chirped from beside her.

Pandora hung her head and turned to leave. It was the worst thing that could happen. If she couldn't communicate with the cats, she and Willa were on their own. Not to mention that she would never have the satisfaction of telling Otis that she could finally talk to her human.

But her last thought was the worst. She could still talk to Fluff. Would she be destined to live out her years with Fluff as the only cat she could communicate with?

CHAPTER FIFTEEN

I felt bad that Pandora still couldn't talk to the barn cats. She brushed it off as if it was no big deal, but her depressed silence on the ride to the bookstore spoke volumes.

"Pepper should be back today. Maybe she knows how to reverse it," I said.

"I'll hold my breath until we see her, then," Pandora said sarcastically. "How did your meeting go? Are you changing the house around? Because if so, I'd like some cat doors."

"I was just thinking about making the bathroom bigger, but I'm not sure now. You know, it's good for one, but…"

"Ah, you're thinking of cohabitating with Striker." Pandora appeared to mull this over. "It's a good idea. You could do much worse, and you're not getting any younger. He's a nice guy, and he likes me. That should be reason enough."

I didn't answer. I wanted to tell her that it was none of her business, but she was already depressed over not being able to talk to the cats, and I didn't want to make her feel worse. There was already a crowd outside the bookstore waiting for it to open, so I pushed my way through, opened it, and sold a bunch of books.

The crowd died down after about an hour, and I was just settling in when the door burst open.

"I have never been more insulted in my life!" Pepper came rushing in and plopped down on the sofa.

"What happened?" I asked. I glanced at Pandora, who had jerked awake and leapt out of her bed to trot over.

"At the herbal conference, Marina Delacroix told everyone that my herbal teas were so messed up that people were coming all the way from Mystic Notch to buy tea from her." Tears swam in Pepper's big green eyes. "Can you believe it?"

"She's probably just jealous." I glanced at Pandora. The cat was living proof that Pepper's teas did tend to have unpredictable results.

"She even named names."

"Who?"

"Nancy Werther, Tom Greenfield, and Felicity Bates, of all people!"

"Speaking of messed-up tea." Pandora jerked her head toward the window.

It didn't appear as if Pepper could understand her, so I spoke up. "Right. Well, speaking of tea, there was a little problem." I tilted my head toward the window.

Pepper looked in that direction, her eyes widening. "It's gone! What happened?"

"Pandora drank it," I said.

"Way to be subtle," Pandora said from her spot on the floor.

"Why?" Pepper asked.

I sat on the sofa beside her. I knew that Pepper believed there were magical forces in Mystic Notch, and nothing I said was probably going to surprise her. But what might surprise her was that this kind of talk was coming from me. I'd resisted all of her efforts to get me on board with the magic. "It's kind of a long story, but I had an old cookbook here, and it apparently contained a magical key."

Pepper frowned, her gaze flicking from Pandora to me. "Wait, you believe in magical keys?"

"Well, I didn't. But certain events have happened that have forced me to believe, and now when I look back, I see all the signs that pointed toward magic here all along. Pepper, you were right. There is magic, and I'm sorry that I doubted you or made light of it before."

Pepper beamed and placed her hand on top of

mine. "It's no problem, Willa. I knew you would come around eventually. Now, tell me what happened."

I told her about Pandora's ability to communicate with me, how Mary had gotten the cookbook and been killed, how the key had gone missing, and how Pandora now couldn't talk to the Mystic Notch cats.

"Someone stole the key from you?" Pepper asked. "We have to find that person!"

"Tell me about it," Pandora said.

"That's become problematic without the help of the other cats," I said.

Pepper scrunched up her face. "Where was the key?"

"In a box on that shelf." I pointed to the shelf.

"And who was here in between the time you put it in the box and the time you noticed it missing?"

"Lots of people. Felicity Bates, various customers, the regulars. I even thought I saw Sarah Delaney running away from the shop when I came back from an appointment, but I can't swear she was inside."

"Oh dear, lots of people that might want an enchanted key." Pepper's face was creased with worry. "This could be very bad. Keys can be used to open portals, and you don't want that to happen."

"So I've heard." I nodded toward Pandora.

Pepper reached out to pat Pandora on the head. "I'm sorry you can't talk to your friends anymore, but it's good you can communicate with Willa." Pepper's eyes slid to the windowsill. "You shouldn't have drunk the tea though. It wasn't for you."

"I think Pandora was hoping that you could do something to reverse the ill effects of the tea," I said. "Oh, and by the way, your little ploy to get me to be more receptive to Striker's hints about moving didn't work because Pandora was the one who drank the tea."

Pepper looked at me in confusion. "What are you talking about?"

"I know you made that tea for me to drink so that I would be more open to Striker. I think he's been hinting a little bit about moving our relationship to the next level."

Pepper snorted. "That tea wasn't for you. Maybe Striker has been hinting. I don't know about that. The tea was for an elderly couple who had lost the ability to communicate over the years. They could still talk to each other, but they just weren't on the same page. I guess it's a good thing they never drank it. Who knows what ill effects it might have had on them." Pepper glanced regretfully at Pandora. "I'm just sorry Pandora had to suffer."

"So, it wasn't for me to drink and get the hint about Striker?" Maybe my plans to renovate my bathroom had been premature.

Pepper laughed. "No, but if you ask me, it would be great if you guys did move your relationship along."

"Enough about your love life," Pandora cut in. "Get her to do something so I can talk to the cats again."

"Can you make another tea that will help Pandora talk to the other cats? Like an antidote tea?" I asked.

Pepper looked doubtful. "I could try to make another tea, but then you risk the problem that she can't talk to you *or* the cats."

Pandora flopped on the floor dramatically. "Oh great, then all I will have is Fluff to talk to."

I ignored the cat. "So, what can be done?"

Pepper looked at Pandora. "I've heard the solution to this sort of thing can be rather drastic, and I'm afraid I don't know of anything in particular." She sighed and slumped in her seat. "Maybe Marina was right about me. Maybe I should give up making magical teas."

"I wouldn't go that far." Actually, it might not be a bad thing, but I didn't want to say that to Pepper. She did love her teas, and not all of them backfired.

"I don't know. The other teas that backfired were minor. But this is a big deal. My tea backfired, and now all of Mystic Notch is in danger. How can I ever concoct a magical tea in good conscience again?"

CHAPTER SIXTEEN

With both my best friend and my cat in a depression and hardly any leads on who took the key, I figured things couldn't get much worse. I figured wrong. Around five p.m., just as I was closing up the shop, Felicity Bates walked through the door.

She looked bad. Like she'd aged twenty years since I'd last seen her. Instead of storming in with her usual venomous manner, she hobbled in with a cane. Her red hair hung damp and lank, devoid of its usual springy curls. Her skin was sallow. Her clothes hung on her bony frame. I'd only seen her two days ago, and she'd deteriorated quite a bit.

But even though Fluff had told Pandora that she was the victim of a misenchantment, I was still suspicious. She could be the one who stole the key and murdered Mary and was now trying to cover her tracks with a clever aging charm. But why would she come here if she'd already stolen the key?

"Willa. We need to talk." She hobbled over to the couch and collapsed as if I wasn't going to kick her out. I wanted to, but I also wanted to hear what she had to say.

Fluff circled around her like a bodyguard protecting a celebrity. Pandora trotted out from behind the counter but kept her distance from Fluff.

"So, we meet again," I heard Pandora say to Fluff. I couldn't make out his answer, just meows.

"I expect by now you know what is going on and how serious the situation here is in town," Felicity said.

"Yes." I didn't elaborate on exactly what I knew. I didn't want to tip my hand to her in case she was up to something.

"As you can see, I am no threat." Felicity gestured to her aged body.

"It looks that way, but looks can be deceiving." I cautiously approached the chair that was farthest away from where she was sitting and sat down.

She gave a wry smile. "I can see why you might think that, given that we have been at odds for so many years after you had my son thrown in jail for murder."

I bit my tongue. She made it sound like I had framed him and he was innocent. The truth was, he was a murderer, and I had only done my duty as a good citizen.

She leaned forward, and I thought I could hear her bones creaking. "I need your help, and I've something to bargain for it."

"That's nice, but I don't actually need anything."

Felicity's gaze flicked over to Pandora. "Maybe you don't, but your cat does."

"You should listen to her," Pandora said.

I didn't know if Felicity could hear Pandora, but I didn't think so, judging by the way she was intently staring at me.

"Okay, I'm listening," I said.

Felicity reached down and buried her fingers in Fluff's fur. He purred, and by the shocked look on Pandora's face, I figured purring wasn't in his usual repertoire. "I heard from Fluff that Pandora is in a bit of a bind. She can no longer talk to the Mystic Notch cats."

I crossed my arms over my chest. "And what of it?"

"I know how she can remedy that."

I narrowed my eyes, still skeptical.

"I think we better hear what she has to say." Pandora's meows had a tinge of desperation.

"How?" I asked.

Felicity leaned back in her chair and chuckled. "Oh no, my body may be fading, but my brain is still working just fine. I'm not going to give away my secrets. First you must promise that you will help me."

Darn. Of course, she knew I would never go back on a promise. But I wanted to know exactly what I was signing up for first. "What is it that you want help with?"

"You have to promise."

"Promise her!" Pandora shouted.

"Okay, I promise."

"Actually, we're after the same thing. I *was* after the key. You were right about that. But I'm not after it so I can bring harm to Mystic Notch. That's where you were wrong. I have only the best interests of the town at heart and always have, but your sour attitude toward me would never let you see it."

"Okay, whatever you say."

"Anyway, we must find the key and the receptacle it opens. If what I suspect is true, then the solution for Pandora and I is the same. She has been the victim of an enchanted tea gone wrong, has she not?"

How had she known that? I doubted that Pandora had told Fluff. The white cat must have found out about Pandora's communication problems somehow and told Felicity, but how had they known it was a tea? Felicity must've seen the startled look in my eyes because her smile widened.

"So, what if she is?" I asked.

"I, too, am the victim of such a thing. I never

should've gone to Marina Delacroix. But luckily, I know how to reverse it."

Ha! So, Marina messed up with her teas as well. I made a mental note to tell Pepper. Hopefully, that would lift her spirits and help her regain her confidence.

Pandora leaned forward, interested in Felicity's every word.

"How?" she meowed.

"How?" I translated for her.

Felicity glanced at Fluff as if for permission to elaborate. The cat nodded. "As you know, the key opens a portal. Normally, you'd think a portal would be a doorway or a grandfather clock, but I happen to know that this particular portal is in a box."

I glanced at Pandora. We were both thinking the same thing—Robert Frost's box.

Felicity continued, "Yes, yes, I know. It's not good to open a portal. All kinds of bad things can happen. But there are certain ways it can be opened, and to take a whiff of portal aroma before anything escapes can reverse a tea potion gone wrong."

I glanced at Pandora. Could it be true? Pandora nodded vigorously.

"It seems dangerous. What if evil creatures escape?"

"That's the tricky part. There may be a way to open it slightly and just take a little whiff then close it quickly. I've heard instructions have been handed down."

"I'm not sure I can trust you. You came here the other day looking for something. Maybe you are just back here now looking for the box that goes with it," I said. "How do I know this is not a trick and that you didn't kill Mary to get the key?"

"She didn't have the key," Felicity said. "Fluff told me the book was torn apart, so whoever killed Mary probably has it. But that wasn't me, and I can prove it."

"How?" Of course, I knew Mary's killer didn't have the key, or at least they hadn't gotten it from Mary, but I wasn't about to tell Felicity that it had been in the box on my shelf at the time. She did seem quite certain that Mary's killer had taken it, which meant she didn't know it had been in the box. If that were the case, then she really didn't have it.

"Gus questioned me about her death. Seems someone told her that I was upset that you sold the recipe book to Mary." Felicity gave me a look indicating that she knew it was me. "But I actually have an alibi for the time of her death."

"I'll bet you do. How do we know that isn't some sort of magical trick? The cops wouldn't know to suspect that."

"Because my alibi is you."

"Me? How?"

"I was here buying a book from you at the time. I

have the receipt. You see, Mary was able to dial 911, and Gus arrived right after the murder. The times are all recorded in her police log."

"You could have killed her and rushed here to create an alibi." But the more I thought about it, the more I realized Felicity couldn't be the killer. She had been mad about the recipe book when she was here, but if she'd killed Mary just before that, she would have already known I'd sold it to her.

"Gus looked in her log. She had found your card in Mary's hand, and while Jimmy was securing the scene, she rushed over here. The log shows how long it takes to get from Mary's to Last Chance Books, and it proves that I wouldn't have had time to kill Mary, change my bloody clothes, and then come here and buy a book."

I thought back to the day in question. She had been sitting leisurely on the sofa. Not out of breath or rushing. I hated to say it, but I was starting to believe her.

"Okay, if this is all true, what do you want me to do?"

"I know you're looking for the key, and now you need to also locate the box. I need the key and the box, as does Pandora. All I am asking is that you let me know when you find it. Give me a chance to get a whiff of portal air along with Pandora. I've already given you what I had to trade—the knowledge of how Pandora can regain her ability to talk to the

Mystic Notch cats. Now, I'm trusting that you'll keep your promise and notify me when you have the key and the box."

I sighed. "Fine. But I can't make any promises about actually finding them."

"I know. But this is my only chance. All I ask is that you put my number in your contacts and text me if you do find them."

Pandora paced the bookstore after Felicity and Fluff left. "I'm not sure we can trust them."

"Me neither," Willa said as she frowned down at her phone. "Felicity is the last person I ever thought I'd have in my contacts, but we don't have any other ideas on how to restore your ability to talk to the cats."

"If the key really was Robert's and it opens the box he kept his poems in, that box could be the portal."

"He described it in detail, so at least we know what it looks like."

"If only I could communicate with the cats, I could send them out looking far and wide for a box that matches the description."

"We may have to wait until Elspeth comes back to town next week. Maybe I can tell her, and she can tell the cats," Willa said.

"A week? I don't know if we have that long. We can't risk the person who has the key finding it first."

Willa glanced out the window. "That's if we can even trust the information we got from Felicity, of course."

"I can't think of any reason for her to make all this up, but we need to proceed with caution," Pandora said. "She didn't lie about one thing. There are instructions about opening a portal."

"There are? That's good, right?"

"Maybe. Right now, they are buried in a safe place and being guarded by the cats."

"Can we get them? If we find the key and the box, you could restore your ability without risking too much. I mean, if what Felicity says is true."

"It won't be that easy. They are buried deep. It's going to be a project that you and I alone can't handle. Unfortunately, I can't ask the cats about this since I can't communicate with them. There might be another way though."

"Oh?"

"Remember Robert said that the box was almost magical for him, but if anyone else opened it, bad things happened?"

"Yes."

"He may be one who is immune to the dire effects of the portal."

"So, he can open it without bad consequences," Willa said. "We might not need those instructions."

"It's possible."

"I'm not sure if we should rule Felicity out entirely, but we do need to start looking into our other suspects. The fact that Fluff was at Mary's does seem to indicate that they don't have the key."

"It does. And she did just give us that tip about the portal air. If that is even true. She looks like crap, though." Pandora hadn't sniffed out any trickery on Felicity. She really was falling apart. "And Fluff does seem distraught about her."

"Yeah, but this whole portal thing seems danger-ous. What if it's really some elaborate trick to let demons out?"

"That's another reason to message her if we find the key and box. If what she says is really true, then she won't mind going first."

That night, Striker stopped by after work. Given what I had found out about the tea, I felt a bit awkward about my assumptions about his intentions.

"Are you getting some work done on the place?" he asked as he took two pieces of ricotta pie out of a bag. My mouth watered. It was from Earline's Diner, and her ricotta was my favorite.

I panicked and blurted out, "No."

He looked at me funny. "Steve Wheeler said he came by."

"Oh, right. I was just thinking maybe the bathrooms are a bit small. Wanted to see what my options were."

Striker handed me a piece of pie. He didn't seem bothered about a potential bathroom renovation.

Maybe he didn't care, or maybe I was making too much of it. Probably the latter.

"Sounds like a good idea. I'm happy to help if you need it."

We settled down in the living room. The paperweight sat uselessly on the coffee table in front of us no matter how many times I looked at it.

Pandora sat at Striker's feet, shooting me knowing glances and then tilting her head toward Striker. "See, he's perfect. He brings pie."

She had a point, but of course I couldn't answer her, so I just smiled at her and made shooing motions. I felt bad for her. She had shown no interest in going to Elspeth's barn, saying "What's the point" in a defeated voice when I had asked her earlier.

"So, how is the case going?" I asked, trying to be subtle.

"Some interesting developments."

That caught my interest. "Really? Anything you can talk about?" I shoved a piece of pie into my mouth. It was rich and creamy, sweet with just a hint of almond.

"It seems like Danielle Norden might not have an alibi after all."

I glanced at Pandora. All this time we'd been focusing on Felicity and hadn't looked into Danielle because we thought she had an alibi. Had Danielle lied? If so, that moved her to the top of my list.

"But what was her motive?" I asked.

"It turns out the two had competing blogs. Recipe blogs or something." Striker waved his hand dismissively as if recipe blogs were of no consequence. "There was some sort of rivalry, I guess, and the fact that Danielle lied about her alibi makes us a little suspicious."

It made me suspicious too. "You think she would kill someone over a blog?"

"It's extreme, but I've seen people kill over less. We need to check it out anyway. She does say a witness saw her leaving Mary's before the time of death."

Probably Jennifer Jones, though Jennifer hadn't mentioned it.

"What about Felicity Bates? I heard Gus questioned her too."

Striker's brow quirked up. "You certainly are up on this case. Do you have an interest in it?"

I shrugged, feigning indifference. "Just making conversation. Mary was a good customer, and I guess I'm just curious."

"We did, but she had the best alibi of all. She happened to be buying a book from you."

"Don't you think that's a little convenient?" I asked. Even though it appeared as if Felicity couldn't be the killer, I still secretly wanted it to be her. I wondered if Felicity could rig the receipt. Maybe she had computer skills or had done it with magic. I couldn't tell Striker about the magic though. He wasn't totally on board with it even though he could see ghosts. But Danielle was a more likely candidate. She had been overly angry about me selling the book to Mary and had lied about her alibi. That pointed to guilt right there. But was Danielle after the key, or did she really want the book for her blog? Looked like I'd be having a little chat with Danielle.

Striker finished his pie, put his plate on the coffee table, then pulled me toward him and gave me a kiss on the side of my head. "Let's look on the bright side. At least we haven't seen any ghosts in this one. Now, enough talk about investigations. We have more important things to do."

AFTER WILLA WENT TO BED, PANDORA SNUCK OUT her usual escape route in the basement. She didn't go to the barn though. Seeing the cats she could no longer talk to was too depressing. There was someplace else that was much more important to her right now. Gladys Primble's backyard.

If only she could obtain the instructions for the portal. They would come in handy if they wanted to try to open it safely, but she couldn't ask the cats to hand them over. Even if she could talk to them, she doubted Inkspot would allow it. And besides, digging them up would require human intervention. They were buried too deep and needed someone with shovels. Felicity was too weak to do it herself, but maybe she had convinced someone to do it for her. Pandora needed to see if they'd been dug up.

It was late at night, and the streets of Mystic Notch were empty. The moon was a crescent in the sky that lit her way. Not that she needed light. Her superior vision enabled her to see practically in the dark.

She stuck to the wooded areas, avoiding the feral cats for fear that she wouldn't be able to talk to them either. She didn't need anything to make her more depressed.

When she got to Gladys Primble's modest house, she discovered she wasn't alone.

Otis was crouched down behind a shrub at the edge of the yard, watching the very spot where the instructions had been buried. No one had been digging, which meant that Felicity didn't have them. Time was running out, and they had no idea how to open that portal box safely.

The last cat she'd wanted to run into right now was Otis, so she turned to run, but he'd spotted her.

"Meow!" he said, probably to needle her about not being able to understand him.

Pandora remained silent.

To her dismay, he trotted toward her. She resisted the urge to run, which would make her look cowardly.

He sat down next to her, looking from her to the yard in an attempt to communicate. Was he trying to communicate without words?

Pandora nodded.

Otis passed his paw over his eyes and then pointed toward the spot. He was trying to tell her that he was keeping watch. Great, now Felicity would never be able to get at the instructions even if she had found a way.

But Otis had no way of knowing how important those instructions were to Felicity and Pandora, and Pandora appreciated his efforts to keep them safe. She bowed her head slightly, hoping it would show her appreciation but not deference.

Otis nodded and pointed back toward the woods, indicating that she didn't need to stay. Either that or he just wanted to get rid of her.

Otis was being nice, and she *did* owe him. After all, he had guzzled down a potion to save her. Lucky thing he hadn't had to resort to the most selfless thing—the breath of life. If he'd done that, they would be bonded for the rest of their nine lives.

She turned to go, but then his paw on her leg stopped her. She turned around and looked at him. She could see sympathy in his fiery orange eyes.

She nodded again, and then she turned and ran.

Somehow the sympathetic gesture from her archenemy was worse than all the other things that had happened to her.

CHAPTER EIGHTEEN

"I thought the article about the bookstore would be in this morning's Gazette," Hattie Dearing said the next morning at the bookstore. She was settled on the purple couch with a Styrofoam coffee cup in front of her and the Gazette opened in her lap.

She pointed to a section of the Gazette where I could see Josie had printed the article on Mary Ashford's blog. "She must've decided to print the article on Mary instead. I guess she was capitalizing on recent events."

"Kind of ghoulish," Cordelia said.

Hattie sighed. "I was looking forward to reading what you said about us."

"That Josie is a bit cutthroat. I guess she is trying to claw her way to the top, but capitalizing on someone's death is not the right way to do it." Cordelia took a sip of her coffee. "She's even getting aggressive. I saw her arguing with Sarah Delaney, trying to force her to give her an interview."

At the mention of Sarah Delaney, Pandora and I both perked our ears up. I hadn't forgotten that I'd thought I'd seen Sarah looking around my shop. Had I checked the box to see if the key was in there after I'd seen Sarah? I didn't think so. I had no reason to check the key at that time. Could Sarah be behind this? There were no clues or evidence linking Sarah to Mary's place, but that didn't mean she wasn't there. And I wasn't forgetting about Felicity either. She was suspicious even in her weakened state. What if the two of them had teamed up?

I was kind of glad the article hadn't been printed today though. Hattie was expecting a big chunk of it to be about her and her sister, but I'd barely mentioned them. She was not going to be happy.

The article was the least of my worries though. Given what Striker had said about Danielle last night, I knew I needed to talk to her right away. Pandora had filled me in about the instructions, and at least no one had dug them up, but maybe that was even worse. If the person who stole the key used it to open a portal without the instructions, that could be disastrous. But of course, if their intentions were nefarious to begin with, they wouldn't be concerned with keeping demons and other undesirable spirits at bay.

I patiently made small talk with the regulars as I

waited for them to leave so I could get Danielle into the store. All the while, Pandora was pacing around, casting furtive glances my way and saying things like, "We should be doing something, time is growing short." By the time the senior citizens left the store, my anxiety was at peak levels.

Once the last of them had shut the door, I turned to Pandora. "I'm going to get Danielle to come here so we can talk to her." I had already told Pandora about Striker's revelation that her alibi had been a lie. Even though they had competing blogs, I doubted Danielle would kill Mary, but why lie about her alibi? Something more was going on.

"Finally!" Pandora said. "I was wondering when you were going to get to that."

I raised my brow at her. She was one to talk. As far as I could see, she'd been spending most of her time lounging around and feeling sorry for herself other than one midnight trip to Gladys Primble's.

She got the hint. "I'm going to do something too. I've decided I can't wallow in my depression. I need to take action, so I'm going to seek out the Mystic Notch cats. Maybe even if I can't talk to them, I can observe them and get a handle on what they are doing and maybe even some clues as to what they have discovered."

I felt sympathetic toward Pandora. She'd told me about seeing Otis the night before. She made light of it, but I knew it had bothered her.

"So, if you'll just let me out the front door." Pandora had trotted over and was looking back at me.

I frowned. I didn't like the idea of letting my cat out. The outside world was dangerous, and all kinds of things could happen. She could get hit by a car or mauled by an animal or get hurt and be lying somewhere, and I wouldn't know to come to her aid.

As if reading my mind, she said, "I can take care of myself out there, trust me. There are plenty of cats around to help out if I run into trouble."

I didn't want to argue with her, and now that we could talk as equals, it didn't feel right to demand she stay inside the shop. I crossed my fingers, hoping what she said was true, and opened the door, my heart squeezing as she trotted away down the street.

I scoured the shelves for an old recipe book that I could use to lure Danielle to the store. I didn't find anything as ancient as the one Mary had bought, but I did find a 1970s version of *The Joy of Cooking*. It would have to do.

I put in a call and waited for her to show up. About an hour later, she came through the door.

"You found another old cookbook?" She looked excited, not like someone who had murdered another person for the previous old cookbook just days before.

"Yes. I mean, it's not as old as the other one, but I thought you might have an interest." I pulled the thick book from under the shelf and put it on the counter. It was a nice hardcover, white with gold letters, about nine hundred pages, and must have weighed a couple of pounds.

Her smile turned into a frown. "This?"

"It's from the 1970s. It's practically an antique," I said.

She kept frowning.

"I know it's not like the really old one I had, but considering…" I let my voice trail off and watched Danielle's expression darken.

"It wasn't fair that Mary got that old one. She didn't deserve it. She's a liar and a thief. She stole recipes from my blog!"

Hm. Could that have been the motive for her murder? Maybe it had nothing to do with magic, keys, or portal. "But you were at her house the day she was killed, so you must not have disliked her that much. Unless you went to argue with her."

Her eyes narrowed. "Did your sister put you up to this?"

I snorted. "Hardly. Gus tries to keep me as far from any investigation as possible." Why did people think that Gus would enlist my aid to interview suspects? It was actually the opposite. I was the last person she would listen to when it came to detective work.

"Well, I was there to argue, but I can prove I didn't have anything to do with Mary's death because someone saw me leaving before Mary was killed."

"Who?"

"Sarah Delaney. She'll remember seeing me, too, because I gave her a piece of my mind."

"You did? Why?" My brain was whirling. Finally, a link between Sarah and Mary! If Danielle was telling the truth, then that might mean that Sarah was at Mary's right before the time that she died. Maybe even during the time she died. But if that was true, why did Danielle lie about her alibi?

Danielle fisted her hands on her hips. "Because you shop owners are the same. You don't play fair. Someone puts their name in for an old book, and you give it to someone else. Sarah is no better than you."

"What do you mean?"

"You're not the only one in town with old books. Sarah has them in her antique store too." Danielle waved at the volume on the counter. "Much older than this thing. Anyway, apparently Mary was desperate for old recipes. She had just paid for a lot of ads to go to her blog, and she needed new recipes. We sort of got into it down at Sarah's the other day, fighting over an old recipe book I found in the back of her shop."

"Okay… so why did Sarah go to Mary's?"

"Don't you see? Mary had probably made a deal

with her, and Sarah was delivering a book. Didn't even bother to offer it to me!"

The wheels in my brain started turning. I'd seen Sarah disappearing down the alley beside my shop the day the key had disappeared. Had the key been in the box after I'd seen Sarah that day? What if she had somehow broken in magically and taken the key? I couldn't remember if I checked the box afterward, but Pandora had been in the store. Surely, she would have noticed Sarah coming in? Could Sarah have put some sort of a sleep spell on the cat?

And of course, it would be just like Sarah to be mixed up in an evil plot to open a portal. She dressed like a witch, thought like a witch, and even smelled like a witch.

"Are you sure Sarah was delivering a book to Mary?"

"Why else would she be sneaking around Mary's house? Plus, she ducked behind a forsythia bush as soon as she saw me. That right there proves she was up to something and didn't want me to know. Don't worry, I gave her a piece of my mind. It was stressful, and that's why I messed up the timing and told your sister I was at the spa."

"Really?" It was hard to believe she would forget arguing with Sarah and tell Gus she was at the spa.

"Yes. It wasn't totally my fault. Gus only asked where I had been around three p.m. My massage appointment was at three, but I had to take the four p.m. slot because arguing with Sarah made me late. But when Gus asked me where I was, I got all flustered and looked in my calendar and saw the massage appointment. I forgot that I had actually been late to it. It's all straightened out with Gus now. I mean, I would hardly be stupid enough to lie about an alibi that could so easily be verified to be false."

"Of course you wouldn't." Could the explanation for the lie really be that simple? Gus could be intimidating, and Danielle wouldn't be the first person to get flustered under her intense questioning.

"So anyway, thanks for calling me, but I don't really want this book. I'm looking for something older," Danielle said.

"Oh okay, well, I'll keep you in mind."

Danielle left, and I stood at the counter to gather my thoughts. Sarah and Felicity had fought at the Cut & Curl. Sarah had been seen near my shop.

Felicity had the receipt proving that she was in my store at the time of death, but I still didn't trust her. Could she fake her haggard appearance with a spell?

Her hair had lost its sheen, she was hunched over, her fingernails were ragged…

Wait! Fingernails!

I glanced up at the box that had held the key. The key had been missing when we had opened it, but it hadn't exactly been empty. There had been a piece of plastic in there that I assumed had been there the whole time, but what if it hadn't?

I rushed to the trash barrel, thankful that I hadn't emptied it yet. I pulled out the little moon-shaped piece of plastic. It wasn't a piece of plastic. It was a fingernail tip. A black fingernail. And who did I know that had black fingernails?

Sarah Delaney.

CHAPTER NINETEEN

I dropped the fingernail in disgust, then scooped it into a baggie with a piece of paper and washed my hands. I locked up the shop and rushed off to Sarah's store. I didn't really have a plan. I didn't know what I was going to do, but by poking around in the store and asking some questions like I had when I was a reporter, I was sure that something would shake loose.

The day had flown by, and it was late afternoon.

Sarah's shop was a couple of blocks away. A group of familiar cats was hanging around in the alley beside the shop. One of them was Pandora.

"You can communicate with them?" I asked hopefully.

"No. But sometimes you don't need words." Pandora still sounded down in the dumps but maybe a little more hopeful.

I remembered a few other times I thought I saw a cat that resembled Pandora near Sarah's. I had always thought she had a doppelgänger, but now I wasn't so sure.

"Was that you I've seen here a few other times?" I asked.

"Me? No." Pandora avoided eye contact. "Don't we have more important matters to discuss? What brings you here?"

I told her about the visit from Danielle and the fingernail I'd found in the wastebasket.

"That wasn't a piece of plastic in the box, and I'm pretty sure it wasn't in there before I put the key in."

"A fingernail? Yuck!"

"Tell me about it." I wiped my hands on my jeans. "What are you doing here? Is something going on?"

"As far as I can tell, the Mystic Notch cats are surveilling Sarah. They've been going around town performing surveillance on our various suspects. That's common in an investigation. Cats can tell a lot of things that people can't, you know."

"No doubt." I looked over the gaggle of cats. To anyone not in the know, they looked like regular cats hanging around in the alley, but I recognized some of them from my many trips to Elspeth's. These were no regular cats. "So, the cats suspect Sarah too? I must be on to something."

"Not so fast," Pandora said. "Look at them."

All the cats were staring up at me and shaking their head as if saying no.

"The person who took the key has to be Sarah. Felicity has an alibi, and Danielle was seen leaving Mary's before she was killed. Who else do we have?"

"Don't forget, the person who killed Mary is a crafty witch. And a good liar. They might be lying to you and also be using magic to fake certain things."

Of course, she was right. Which meant that Felicity could have been faking her ailment. I wouldn't put it past her. But Sarah could be lying too. Striker hadn't mentioned her as one of the suspects. Did the police even know she'd been to Mary's? Surely Danielle had mentioned it.

"I still think it's important to check out Sarah. She might know something even if she isn't the person." I still thought Sarah really was the person but wanted to appease Pandora.

I opened the door to the shop and looked back at my cat. "You coming?"

Pandora glanced at the other cats who were still shaking their heads. She shrugged and followed me into the store.

The antique store was crammed full of old furniture and smelled like lemon Pledge. Shelves full of items lined the middle of the store. They were loaded with various kinds of glassware, silver teapot sets, and other antique items. Sarah had increased the inventory since I'd last been in there, and it was so crowded you could barely see if anyone else was in there.

As soon as we entered, Sarah's little Yorkie came rushing out of nowhere, dancing around on the faded blue-and-red oriental rug and yipping at Pandora.

"Oh no! I can understand its little noises more clearly now." Pandora turned to the small dog, arched her back, and hissed. "Shut up."

"Yipe!" The dog tucked its tail between its legs and ran behind a three-foot-tall Ming vase.

"Oh, I guess it can understand me too," Pandora said.

Sarah came rushing out from somewhere in the bowels of the store. "Skeezits! What happened?" She rushed toward the dog, stopping short when she saw me. "Oh, Willa. What are you doing here in the middle of the day? Shouldn't you be tending to your shop?"

"I'm not the only one that leaves my shop in the middle of the day, Sarah. Didn't I see you running away from my shop the other morning?"

Sarah glanced down at Skeezits, who was panting up at her. She scooped him up and planted a kiss on top of his head. "I don't know what you mean."

"I think you do. You were after the key, weren't you?" I decided to just go for it. There was no point in beating around the bush.

"I wasn't after any key. I don't know what you're talking about."

"I think you do, and I think you're up to something. That's why you fought with Felicity about spices in the Cut & Curl the other day. That fight wasn't about spices. It was about the cookbook and where the key was hidden, wasn't it?"

Sarah looked genuinely surprised. "The key was hidden in a cookbook? How interesting. But you're wrong about the argument. We actually were arguing about spices. You see, we had made the same toad-spiced pumpkin bread for the witches' bake-off."

Toad spiced? Witches' bake-off? I made a disgusted face.

"Yeah, it's a thing. Anyway, there was a question about whose dish was best. I say the savory spices made mine the better one. She thinks her sweet one was better."

"There's a witches' bake-off?"

"Yeah. Second Sunday in August, midnight, in the clearing behind the bowling alley. I'm surprised you didn't know about it. I saw your ghosts, Robert and Franklin, there."

"How did you know I had ghosts? I didn't think they actually ever left the shop." As far as I knew, Pandora and I were the only ones that they talked to. Pepper knew about them because I had told her, but I hardly thought she would be telling Sarah.

"They usually don't, but they are allowed to manifest at certain witch gatherings. Other than that, it's just your shop and the ghostly realm. Not many people know, but I happen to be able to communicate with ghosts. Robert and Franklin are just delightful, and they were quite keen to have some dishes named after them."

"Yeah, I'd heard that." Why was Sarah going off on a tangent like this? Was she trying to distract me? "But I don't think you're telling the truth. I think you were in my shop, and that's how you met them."

She frowned. "No. I've never been in there. Would love an invite though."

"Really? Then how do you explain this?" I pulled the plastic bag with the black fingernail tip out of my pocket.

She peered at it then made a face. "Is that my fingernail?"

"I found it in the box where the key was kept. You must have lost it when you stole the key. How did you get in without Pandora noticing?"

Sarah put Skeezits gently on the floor and held up her fingers—short nails. "Wrong again. I had to have Margie at the Cut & Curl cut my nails short because of that argument with Felicity Bates. I was in the middle of a manicure, and my beautiful nails got ruined!"

I crossed my arms over my chest. "A likely story."

"It's true." Sarah turned her hands around to look at her nails, her expression full of regret. "I loved my long nails. These things take forever to grow. You are right about one thing, though. I was at your shop that morning. But I wasn't stealing anything. I didn't go in. That would be rude. I'd heard about the key but had no idea it was in an old cookbook. I was putting a charm on your lock so someone else wouldn't be able to open it with magic and steal the key. Guess that didn't work so good."

Back when I was a journalist, I'd had an uncanny ability to tell when people were lying. Maybe my instincts were off, but I got the feeling Sarah was telling the truth. I glanced over at Pandora to get her take on it, but she was no longer sitting at my feet.

"Willa, I think you should check this out." Pandora's voice came from a few aisles over.

"I'm kind of busy." Was Pandora shopping? We needed to focus on finding out what Sarah was up to and figure out if she was telling the truth, not browse the store for trinkets.

"It's really important and has to do with the magical key."

Oh! Why hadn't she said that in the first place? I proceeded into the store toward the direction of her voice.

Pandora was standing on her hind legs, her front paws on a shelf, looking at a box.

The box was about the size of a bread box. It had a gorgeous tiger maple veneer with ivory inlay and a gold strip around the edge.

"Robert's Frost's box," I said.

Pandora looked up at me. "I think the cats might

have been right. If this is Robert's box and Sarah has the key, why wouldn't she have opened it?"

Sarah came around the corner, Skeezits close on her heels.

"What is it?" she asked.

Pandora looked up at her "As if you didn't know!"

She looked curiously at Pandora. "Is your cat trying to say something to me?"

Skeezits pawed at Sarah. "Yip yip yip."

She turned to Pandora. "As if I didn't know what?"

Apparently Skeezits had translated Pandora's words. If we let the animals in on this conversation, things were going to get complicated.

"We think it's the portal that the key goes to."

"The portal?" Sarah picked the box up carefully. "I could never get this box unlocked no matter how many skeleton keys I tried. I should've known there was something special about it."

"Yip yip yip." The little dog's yipping was getting on my nerves. At least Pandora's meows weren't as loud.

Sarah's gaze jerked to Pandora. "Your cat needs to get it open to reverse a potion gone wrong."

"How did you know that?"

"Skeezits. He knows everything that's going on. He's very intuitive. He saw that the cats and Pandora could no longer communicate, and I happen to know that getting a whiff of the initial air from a portal opening is the only thing that will fix a backfired potion."

"Well, supposedly Pandora's not the only one that needs that. Felicity Bates claims that she needs it too. Are you in cahoots with her?"

Sarah laughed. "Cahoots? Who says that anymore? No, I'm not working with her if that's what you're asking, and I don't have the key." She looked at me seriously. "Willa, this is very serious. If the wrong person opens this, I hate to think what will happen to Mystic Notch."

"Yes, I've heard." I wasn't sure if I could trust Sarah, but if she had the key and the box, she would have opened it already.

"But what does this have to do with Robert Frost?" Sarah asked.

I told her the story of how Robert Frost had kept his poems in the box.

"So, he's a buffer," Sarah said after hearing how his sister and friend had bad luck when they opened the box, but not Robert. "I've heard that there are certain magical people who can open a portal without ramifications. Robert must be one of them."

"That was when he was alive, but we don't know if his ghost has the same ability," I pointed out.

Sarah looked at me intently. "Maybe he does, or maybe he doesn't, but either way we can use this box to flush out the person who has the key. It's critical that we find that person and get the key before they use it."

That sounded very heroic, but I wasn't really sure I wanted part of it. Then again, I didn't want Mystic Notch to become overrun with demons and evil intentions.

"How?" I squeaked out.

She held the box out to me. "You take this box back to your shop. Let everyone see you carrying it. The person that has the key might recognize it and could come to your shop hoping to open it."

"Why don't you just keep it here and put it in your display window or something?" I asked. Seemed like Sarah would be better equipped to deal with the key-holder, whatever that entailed.

Sarah shook her head, her expression serious. "We need to have it in your shop because that's where Robert is. If he truly is a buffer and the key-holder gets the box open, his presence will help mitigate any disastrous effects."

"Really?" I was skeptical.

"Sure. You said so yourself. When his sister and friend opened it, bad things happened but not evil-demon bad. So even if someone else opens it and he's around, it could be the thing that saves Mystic Notch."

"But we're not even sure that will work the same now that he's a ghost." But if it did work, that could be the thing that allowed Pandora to get a first whiff without harm coming to the town.

"What other choice do we have?" Sarah shoved the box toward me, her eyes pleading. "Please take it. I'll keep watch and be ready to help if anything happens."

"I think we have to do it," Pandora said.

I looked down at my cat. She was depending on me. I took the box from Sarah, and Pandora and I went back to my shop to wait.

CHAPTER TWENTY

The waiting was the hardest part. I texted Felicity. Even though I didn't have the key, I did have the box, and just in case she had been lying, it would draw her here. If she hadn't been lying, well, I'd given my word, and if the person with the key did show up, then maybe Felicity could get her whiff of portal air and have her health restored.

Pandora and I sat on the purple sofa, staring at the box.

The door was unlocked, but the sign said closed. We'd turned off all the lights so no customers would come and so that it would be inviting for the person who had the key to break in. Hopefully, the unlocked door would ensure that nothing actually got broken. Though if the person was magical, they could probably get in anyway.

"Maybe the door being unlocked will make them suspicious," I said.

Pandora glanced over. "Maybe. We should see if we can get Robert to appear. We don't want to have to waste time trying to summon him if our adversary comes with the key. There may not be a second to waste."

I nodded. "If someone puts that key in the lock, it could be lights out for all of us."

I glanced at the box again. It looked so innocent just sitting there. It hadn't done anything to indicate that it was a portal to the underworld. No jerky movements, glowing lights, or eerie noises.

"Maybe Robert can verify that this actually is the right box."

We went to the poetry section, and I slid an old leather-bound compilation of Robert Frost poems out of its slot and started leafing through the pages. "Gosh, I hope I don't tear any of these old, brittle pages. I would hate to ruin one of Robert Frost's poems," I said to the ether.

Within seconds, Robert's ghostly apparition swirled in front of me. Franklin followed right behind him.

"Willa! What are you doing? Be careful with that book!" Robert looked dismayed. "Why is that out on the regular shelf? Shouldn't it be under lock and key with other precious books?"

"Oh, don't be such an old fussbudget, Bobby," Franklin said.

"Maybe it should," I said truthfully. I didn't actually have a place to lock up precious books. The book was pretty old, but the pages weren't as brittle as I had been making out.

"Robert, while you're here, we want to show you something." Pandora jerked her head to the front of the store and trotted in that direction. Robert looked at me, and I pointed toward her, indicating for him to follow. He swirled over to the front. His face lit up in pleasure when he saw the box. "It's my poem box!"

"Yay," Pandora said in a flat tone. I couldn't tell if she was excited or worried.

"See, Franklin, I really did have a box." Robert reached out to touch it, and unlike most other objects, his hand didn't pass right through it. This was a good sign. He could actually touch the box! He picked it up and turned it over. Then he turned to me. "Where is the key? I must open it."

"That's the problem. We don't have it."

Franklin and Robert both looked confused. "Yes, you do. It was here earlier. Fell out of that big old recipe book."

"Someone stole it."

"Stole it? Why? Do they think I left some poems in here?" Robert looked thoughtful. "*Did* I leave something here? It's hard to remember."

"I think they want it for another reason," Pandora said.

"What other possible reason would they…" Robert's sentence trailed off, and he squinted toward the window. "Oh, who is that?"

I turned around just in time to see Felicity Bates enter the store, Fluff at her side.

Felicity's eyes drifted to the box and widened. She pointed her bony, gnarled finger toward the box. "That's the portal, isn't it?"

Robert scoffed. "Portal? What is she talking about?"

Felicity didn't answer. Apparently, she could neither see nor hear the ghosts.

Pandora took the opportunity to explain to Robert. "This is where we need your help. Apparently, your box has magical powers. Remember all the times you said other people opened it and had bad luck?"

"Yes." Robert nodded.

"Well, there was a reason for it. Magic. We think you can open it without ill effects, and we're going to need you to do that for us." Pandora and Felicity both had the same hopeful look on their faces.

"Is your cat talking to someone? A ghost perhaps?" Felicity asked.

I explained about Robert Frost's ghost and how the box had belonged to him. Felicity took it in stride. "We think he's a buffer and can open the box so you and Pandora can get a whiff of portal air without releasing anything evil."

She nodded vigorously. "Yes, yes. We need him to help us. Open the box." She took a step forward and collapsed on the floor.

CHAPTER TWENTY-ONE

"Look out, it's a trick!" Pandora yelled as Willa rushed to pick Felicity up off the ground.

Too late. Willa was already there, helping Felicity to her feet and getting her situated on the couch. Pandora braced herself for some sort of a hex to hurt Willa, but nothing came.

"Thank you." Felicity's eyes fluttered. She touched Willa's arm, and Pandora got ready to spring and claw her eyes out if anything bad happened to her human. But all she saw was actual gratitude in Felicity's eyes.

"I'm grateful to your human." Fluff shot a glance at Pandora then jumped up on the couch and sniffed at Felicity, nudging his head under her hand. She started petting him, a small smile flitting across her lips.

"Watch out, Willa. They could be up to something," Pandora said, but she wasn't actually sure that they were up to anything. If they had wanted to do something, they could've done it by now surely. They wouldn't need these theatrics.

"Can I get you some water or anything?" Willa had distanced herself a bit from Felicity on the couch but was still being her helpful self.

Felicity waved away Willa's offer. "No, I'm fine. Do you know who has the key?"

"No idea," Willa said.

Felicity glanced at the box again. "Where did you get this box?"

"Sarah Delaney."

Felicity gasped. "Sarah? But she's not to be trusted."

Neither are you, Pandora thought.

"I believe that box is the portal. Why would she give it to you, and where did she get it?" Felicity asked.

"I don't know where she got it, but I do know why she gave it to me. She hoped it would flush out the person who has the key," Willa said.

"Oh no." Felicity sat up straighter, glancing around the room. "It could be a trick."

"Why would Sarah want to play a trick? She had the box, so if she also had the key, why wouldn't she just open the box with it?"

"Maybe she needed your ghost to protect herself from the effects of the portal."

Willa glanced around uneasily. "Maybe you have a point."

Now Pandora wasn't sure who the bad guy was. And it didn't bode well that Sarah Delaney had said she knew Robert and Franklin. She denied being here in the bookstore, but it did seem weird that Robert and Franklin would go to a witches' bake-off in the woods. Then again, they had been arguing about recipes named after them.

"This is not good. This is really not good." Fluff glanced nervously at the door. "Sarah Delaney scares me, and if she comes here, I hope she doesn't bring that little dog."

"That's one thing we agree on," Pandora said.

Felicity grabbed Willa's arm, her ragged nails digging into Willa's flesh. "Willa, we must find the key."

Fluff jumped down from the sofa to stand in front of Pandora. "We will be forever in your debt if you help us." Fluff sounded desperate.

Pandora admired his dedication to his human. It was unthinkable, but perhaps they weren't pulling a fast one. Could it be that Felicity truly needed a whiff from the box as much as Pandora did? She could relate to that sort of desperation. But the thought that they were suddenly allies was disturbing.

"Please find the key," Fluff begged.

"Do you mean this key?" The voice came from the doorway. They all whirled around to see Josie Martin holding up a glowing blue skeleton key.

CHAPTER TWENTY-TWO

I stared at the door in disbelief. Josie Martin had stolen the key? Not Felicity. Not Sarah. Josie. But then it all started to make sense.

"How did you get in here without the bells over the door chiming?" I asked.

"Bell sleep charm," Josie and Felicity said at the same time.

"Wait, are you in on this together?" I stared at Felicity in disbelief. Had I fallen for her ruse?

She shook her head violently. "No. But I know about the spell. I used it to come in one day myself."

The day I had been talking to Pandora in the back room and she had appeared on the sofa. "So that explains how you got in that day I was out back with Pandora."

"Yeah, it's easy on inanimate objects. Not so much on people though," Felicity croaked out. Her voice was barely above a whisper now, and she was slumped over on the couch. She was getting worse before my eyes. At her feet, Fluff let out a panic-stricken meow. I didn't know what he said, but Felicity reached down and patted his fur as if to reassure him.

"It might be difficult for you, Felicity, but it's easy for me to put the spell on people." Josie walked toward them, her dark eyes glowing maliciously. She still had the skeleton key held up in front of her, the color of its glow changing as she walked closer to the box. White. Blue. Purple.

Robert swirled and clapped his hands in glee. "My key!"

"How did you get the key?" I asked Josie. At least she had stopped at the edge of the couch. I had to figure out a way to prevent her from putting that key in the lock. Behind the box, Robert swirled happily, unaware of the danger just in front of him. Beside me, Felicity tensed. I figured she was thinking about stopping Josie too.

But in her weakened state, Felicity wasn't going to be much help in a physical confrontation. Even if I tackled Josie to the ground, I wasn't sure I'd be able to keep her there. And apparently Josie was magic, so it wouldn't be a fair fight.

"I came in and stole it, of course," Josie said. "Once I discovered it was no longer in the book that Mary bought from you, I knew it had to be somewhere in the shop. Just a simple locator spell with some saffron dust and a sleep spell on you and your cat allowed me to locate the key and grab it without you even knowing."

I stared at her in horror, remembering how sleepy Pandora and I had both been after she came to take pictures for the article. She had taken pictures everywhere, even behind the counter where the box was.

I guess that explains why the article wasn't in the paper. "So, your article on my shop was a fake?" I asked.

Josie shrugged. "I do whatever I have to do to get the job done."

"You did a sleep spell on Willa?" Felicity gave a low whistle. "That's some good magic."

Josie turned to Felicity with a gloating expression on her face. "You should be familiar with it. I did it on you too."

Felicity looked confused. "You did? When?"

"Down at the Cut & Curl. When you and Sarah were arguing about recipes, I cast a sleep spell. I figured I might need to leave some evidence around pointing to someone else should I have to resort to drastic measures to get the key."

"What kind of evidence?" I asked.

"Fingernails." Josie laughed. "Yes, it's kind of gross, but they make great evidence to leave at crime scenes. Then I figured if I was going to steal the key from you, I would leave something that pointed in someone else's direction. It actually ended up working pretty good because it sent you over to Sarah, and Sarah gave you the box."

"How do you know Sarah gave it to me?" I asked.

"I was watching, of course. I knew Sarah had the box in her shop. My plan was to pretend I was doing an article on her and cast a sleep spell so I could steal it. But she wouldn't grant me an interview, and she has wards on her locks that I couldn't get around, so I couldn't get in magically after hours," Josie said. "I left a fingernail at Mary's crime scene, too, so the police will focus on her and not me. Maybe that will take care of Sarah Delaney for good. That would probably make all three of us happy, wouldn't it?"

Maybe I would've said yes a few days ago, but now I felt a little bit of a bond with Sarah. She'd given me the box so that we could flush out the evil perpetrator. Though it would have been nice if she came to help us out like she'd said she would.

"And now what do you intend to do?" I asked.

"Open the box and see what happens, of course. Soon your idyllic town will be turned into something much less agreeable, and I will be in the center of it all!" Josie bent toward the box, aiming the key for the keyhole.

Robert swirled over the box. "You're probably hoping to see some of my poems in there. I think you might be disappointed."

Josie couldn't hear him, of course. The key

turned dark in her hand, and she hesitated for just a second, frowning down at the malevolent-looking key.

It was now or never. I had to do something to stop her. I had to push her away from the box.

"No!" Felicity and I shouted at the same time. We both leapt toward Josie, except Felicity was so weak that she ended up on the floor. I tripped over her, and Josie smiled down at us and laughed as she shoved the key toward the lock.

"Meroooo!" Fluff screeched and launched himself onto Josie's back.

"Ouch!" Josie straightened. The key clattered to the floor as she reached behind her to try to dislodge the cat who was digging his claws into her flesh.

She whirled around, knocking a chair over, stumbling toward the bookshelves, pulling books off the shelf as she scrambled to get rid of the cat. There was a cacophony of screeches and meows as Fluff held on.

On the ground underneath me, Felicity stirred and grunted. Her hand stretched out for something.

The key! It lay on the floor where Josie had dropped it. I grabbed it and handed it to Robert, who was watching Josie and Fluff with much confusion on his face.

"I say, these humans are an odd lot nowadays, don't you think, Franklin?" Robert asked.

"Indeed. What sort of dance is that?" Franklin shook his head.

"Never mind that," I said, shoving the key in Robert's direction. "Open the box!"

"Oh, gladly." Robert took the key. I was surprised he was able to hold it since most things passed through his ghostly hands, but that just proved all the more how magical it was. He leaned down toward the box and put the key in the lock. It glowed gold.

Snick!

The box popped open.

I held my breath, waiting for a demon or maybe a gaggle of bats to fly out or a dark cloud to descend on the town, but nothing like that happened. Lavender-tinted mist wafted out of the box, bringing with it the scent of lily of the valley. That couldn't indicate anything bad, could it?

"Hey, let's not forget why we're here," Pandora reminded me.

I motioned for Robert to put the box in front of her. "Let Pandora get a whiff."

Robert moved toward Pandora, but she waved him off. "Felicity first." She jerked her head in Felicity's direction.

Robert swirled down to the floor and held the box under Felicity's nose. Felicity took in a deep breath then pushed the box toward Pandora.

Pandora twitched her whiskers, closed her eyes, and sniffed as the lavender mist curled around her nostrils.

"Get off me, you menace!" Josie rammed her back into the tall bookcase, lodging Fluff loose.

Fluff flew through the air. "Meooooouch!"

Thud.

He landed on the ground in front of the counter and remained still.

"Fluff!" Felicity rushed over to him and collapsed on the floor beside him. She was already starting to look better, her hair taking on a glossy sheen and curling in corkscrews as I watched. Her skin appeared to be getting younger, her complexion more dewy, and her wrinkles were disappearing. She threw herself down beside the white cat.

Josie whirled around, glaring at me. "You are going to be sorry!"

She lunged toward the box, which Robert was still holding, but because she couldn't see ghosts, it must've looked like it was floating in thin air to her.

"Oh, no, you don't!" Robert jerked the box away from her.

"What the heck?" She looked confused, but she quickly lunged after it again, this time managing to grab on to the corner.

I had to do something. Felicity was no use since she was sobbing over Fluff. I readied for battle. Because Josie was magical, I had no idea what she could do to me, but I had to do something.

Thwack!

Just as I was about to leap toward Josie, the heavy

volume of *The Joy of Cooking* that I had been showing to Danielle hit Josie in the back of the head, and she crumpled to the ground.

I turned toward the front of the store to see Sarah Delaney brushing off her hands. She shrugged. "Door was open, so I thought I'd help out, and that book was the only thing handy. Sorry if I ruined it."

"Thanks. No problem. It was for a good cause." I looked down at Josie, who was out cold.

Sarah approached Robert. "Now maybe you can close the box carefully and give it to Willa."

"Hi, Sarah! Sure. It didn't have any of my poems in it anyway." Robert snapped the box shut and handed it to me along with the key.

I slipped the key in my pocket and clutched the box to my chest, feeling a huge sense of relief. It was over. We'd saved Pandora, Felicity, and the town.

But my joy was short-lived when a mournful wail came from the other side of the sofa where Felicity was still on the floor, clutching a limp Fluff in her arms, tears streaming from her face. "He's not breathing!"

CHAPTER TWENTY-THREE

Pandora approached Fluff cautiously, searching for signs of life. His body was still, his white fur less glossy and full. His whiskers drooped. His chest was not moving. She sniffed at him.

She should have been elated. Her biggest enemy, vanquished! Why did her heart feel so heavy?

Felicity's sobs were getting louder. Judging by the way she was overreacting, you'd think Fluff had only one life. But of course, there was only one he could spend with Felicity.

And looking at the limp body in Felicity's arms, Pandora knew that life was over.

Fluff had given his life to protect his mistress and Mystic Notch. Pandora didn't know how much of that was about the town, but giving up his life to protect Felicity was worth something, wasn't it? He had been an admirable foe, and the truth was, she actually kind of missed him.

But he was already halfway to his new life, and there was only one way to bring him back.

Pandora would have to give him the breath of life.

Once she did, they'd be bonded for all nine of their lives. The thought of that was repugnant, but she also couldn't stand the wailing coming from Felicity, and she felt a certain obligation to help them because in the end they had helped Pandora and Willa. If Felicity had never mentioned the way to reverse a potion gone bad, Pandora would not have had this chance. Of course, she didn't know if it had really worked. She'd have to wait until she could try to talk to the Mystic Notch cats, but judging by the way Felicity was looking pretty much like her old self, she was hopeful her communication with the cats would be restored.

Pandora let out a big sigh and crept over to Fluff's lolling head.

I might live to regret this, but what the heck.

She took a deep breath, bent toward Fluff's pink nose, and breathed out.

"WHAT ARE WE GOING TO DO NOW?" SARAH STARED down at Josie. She appeared to be out cold, but for how long?

I clutched the box to my chest, still afraid it would fly open on its own.

At least Felicity had stopped wailing. I was a little concerned about her cat but didn't have time to think about it right now. Instead, I was thinking about Gus and the murder investigation. Josie was the real killer, as she'd confessed to us, but would Gus be able to figure that out without knowing the paranormal motive?

I didn't think that Sarah had heard Josie's admission that she'd left fingernails at Mary's to throw the police off track. If Gus started to suspect Sarah, I would have to tell Gus that Josie had done that. It wasn't fair to Sarah to let her fall under suspicion. Though she actually had been there that day, and it might not bode well for her if Gus's radar started pointing in her direction.

But how could I make Gus see that Josie was the killer? She certainly would never take my word for it. There would have to be enough corroborating evidence to make her think she thought of it herself.

"Merooo!"

"Meowsa!"

"Mpuurup!"

Outside on the sidewalk, a gaggle of cats had

accumulated. I recognize them as the cats from Elspeth's barn. What were they doing here? As I was looking out, Gus's police car screeched to a stop at the curb.

She stormed toward the bookstore, shooing cats out of her way. She burst through the door, scowling over her shoulder at the cats. "Darn cats are following me everywhere…" Her voice trailed off as she turned and took in the scene.

It must've looked a little strange. Felicity holding a limp Fluff, Pandora doing something I wasn't quite sure of near Fluff's head, and me clutching a box while Sarah stood over an unconscious Josie.

"What in the world?" The way Gus's gaze was flicking from Josie to me and the suspicious look on her face had me thinking she suspected that I was up to something.

"She attacked us!" I pointed toward Josie. "She confessed to killing Mary, and she hurt Felicity's cat."

Gus spun around to look in the direction I was pointing. My mouth flew open in shock as I saw Fluff moving. He clawed his way out of Felicity's grasp and struggled to a sitting position then started preening himself, casting angry glares around as if warding off our sympathy.

"Oh, Fluff, you're okay!" Felicity grabbed the cat and crushed him to her bosom. He did not look pleased.

"I knew it! I had just finished putting the evidence together against Josie. She lied to me about the time she was at Mary Ashworth's. At first, I thought it was Danielle lying about the time. She'd mixed that up before. But when I looked at the article on Mary in the Gazette, I saw that Josie had made a fatal mistake."

"What was that?" Sarah asked.

"The photo in the article had Mary's grandfather clock in the background, which happened to show the time was ten minutes before Mary's death. Josie had said she'd left an hour before." Gus turned and frowned out the window at the cats. "I was just putting it all together in my office when right out of the blue, I had the overwhelming thought that I should come here."

Could the cats have been communicating with her, putting thoughts in her head to come here? Given everything that had happened this week, I wouldn't be surprised.

Gus stood over Josie, who was just starting to stir. She took out her cuffs and slapped them on her wrists. "Josie Martin, you're under arrest for the murder of Mary Ashford."

She hauled Josie to her feet and marched her toward the door. When she got to the door, she turned back, a frown on her face. Her gaze skipped from me to Sarah to Felicity. "Just what are you all doing in here at this time of night anyway? I thought you guys didn't even like each other."

Felicity, Sarah, and I all exchanged a glance, and then at the same time we all blurted out, "Weekly book club."

"And then what happened?" The cats sat in a circle in Elspeth's barn, their attention riveted on Pandora as she regaled them with the account of the capture.

Pandora hadn't wanted to leave Willa, but Striker had rushed over and the two of them got all mushy, so Pandora was glad to escape. Besides, she wanted to know if breathing the portal air had worked.

"Then, Felicity was gushing and crying and holding Fluff."

"Are you quite sure he was dead?" Sasha asked.

Pandora nodded solemnly.

"Good riddance," Hope said. Pandora couldn't blame her. The small chimera was usually very generous hearted, but Fluff had tried to kill her.

"And then what happened?" Otis asked.

Pandora paused and surveyed the audience for effect. "I had to give him the breath of life."

The cats gasped. "Fluff? Why would you?"

"I don't know what came over me. Felicity was crying, Josie was collapsed on the floor, and Sarah had appeared out of nowhere. There were a lot of things going on, and to tell you the truth, it seemed like Fluff had mellowed. If it wasn't for Felicity and Fluff, I never would've regained the ability to talk to you guys."

"Still, it seems like with Fluff out of the picture, things would be a lot easier for us," Kelley, the Maine Coon, said as she groomed her fluffy tail.

"I wouldn't be too sure about that," Pandora said. "Fluff seems to be truly changed. And now he owes me. Perhaps we can work this to our advantage."

The other cats murmured their disagreement, but Inkspot cut in. "Now, now. Let's not be hasty. With Fluff on our side, we could finally figure out some of the items that need to be collected in order to keep Mystic Notch out of danger. After all, he does have part of that list."

"I wouldn't trust him. It's probably a trick," Hope said.

"Be that as it may," Otis said, "the deed is done. Pandora has given him back his life, and now we must deal with whatever ramifications come our way."

Pandora had told her story, but now she had questions for the cats. "I saw all of you outside the shop window. How did you know something was going on?"

"When we saw you at Sarah Delaney's, we knew something was afoot," Tigger said. "Of course we followed you to see if we could help out."

"But not all of us," Inkspot said. "Some of us went to the police station to try to make sure Gus would show up just in case."

That explained why Gus had had the sudden urge to go to Last Chance Books. Even though she had figured out Josie was the killer, she wouldn't have known where to locate her. "It was good you did that. You might have just helped save the town."

Inkspot shrugged. "All in a day's work. And now that the box and key are safe, we can take a little bit of a catnap."

"Meow! Meow!"

"I have dibs on the comfy cat bed!" Sasha raced to the back of the barn.

"Don't get too comfortable," Inkspot called out as he curled up atop a bale of hay. "I have a feeling it won't be long before our services are needed again."

STRIKER HAD RUSHED OVER TO MY HOUSE AS SOON AS he had heard about the incident with Josie. It felt good that he was so concerned about me.

I'd just been putting together a snack of Triscuits,

jalapeños, and cream cheese for us when Gus pulled in. She'd warned me that she would swing by my place to take a statement after she'd booked Josie.

Pandora slipped in the door along with Gus, and I shot her an anxious look. She'd gone to Elspeth's barn, and I was anxious to find out if she could talk to the cats. She nodded, and I smiled. All was getting back to normal. Well, except for the fact that I could now have conversations with my cat.

"So, you're in a book club with Felicity Bates and Sarah Delaney?" Gus grabbed a Triscuit and popped the whole thing in her mouth. "I thought you guys didn't like each other."

"We all like books, so I guess that trumps our dislike of each other." It was a lame excuse, and judging by the skeptical look on my sister's face, she wasn't quite buying it. I didn't really like lying to Gus, but it was best for all.

"Uh-huh. And Josie was in the book club too?"

"Oh no. She wasn't in the club."

"So, what was she doing there?"

"She just came walking in. Apparently, she saw us all in there seated on the sofa discussing our book. She got all angry. I don't know what's wrong with her, but if she killed Mary over a cookbook, maybe she has issues." Felicity, Sarah, and I had discussed our story so that when Gus questioned us, we would all say the same thing about the book club.

Gus's eyes narrowed. "What book were you discussing?"

"*A Discovery of Witches* by Deborah Harkness."

"Hm. Good book."

"It is." I was curious about what Josie had told Gus. It went unsaid that magical folks didn't let on about their abilities to non-magical folks. "So, what happened with Josie? Did she say why she killed Mary?"

Gus frowned. "I think you're right about her having issues. Apparently, she was mad about the recipes on Mary's blog. Said Mary had cheated or something. She even ripped up the recipe book Mary was using. We found it in tatters at the scene of the crime," Gus said. "She said it was a crime of passion."

She glanced at Striker, who was seated at the kitchen table. "Did you know about this book club?"

"I don't know everything Willa does, but if she says she's in a book club, it must be true." Striker winked at me. Of course, I'd never mentioned anything about a book club to him because it didn't exist. It felt good that he was on my side and automatically stuck up for me with Gus. Then it felt bad that I had to let that little white lie exist between us.

Gus rolled her eyes. "Okay, well, Felicity and Sarah say the same thing, so as weird as it seems, I guess you guys have a book club and Josie just busted in. She's still a little vague about why she attacked you though."

I shrugged. "Like I said. She has issues."

Gus studied me while she crunched down another Triscuit. "Okay, well then, I guess that's that. See you two later."

Gus left, and I turned my attention to Striker. "Thanks for sticking up for me. What's in the bag?" I pointed to the shopping bag he'd brought in with him. Hopefully it was some sort of desert, maybe a chocolate cake or peanut butter cookies.

He came to stand next to me at the counter and opened the bag and started rummaging around in it. My mouth watered.

"Tile samples." He lined up some samples on the counter.

"Oh." There was quite an assortment. One was a nice white subway tile, one was aqua iridescent, and another was a limestone in earthy tones. Chocolate cake would have been nice, too, though.

"If you're getting your bathroom done, I thought maybe we could pick them out together. After all, I do spend a lot of time here." He pulled me close and stole a kiss.

"Gross," Pandora piped in from her cat bed, where she'd curled up as soon as she'd come in.

Striker only heard meows. "Are you hungry?" he asked. "I thought maybe we could go out to that steak place."

"Sure!" With all the activity, I hadn't eaten dinner and was starving. I loved steak, and they had a great triple-layer chocolate cake.

"Good. Let's head out, and then later on we can look at these tile samples in the bathroom. Of course, it's up to you what you want, but if you want someone to bounce ideas off of, I'm all yours." I loved how Striker was offering to help but not being pushy with ideas. If I did renovate the bathroom, would that mean he would come over more? I wasn't sure how I felt about that. More time with Striker wasn't a bad thing, but moving in? I wasn't quite ready for that.

CHAPTER TWENTY-FIVE

*P*andora and I opened up the shop as usual the next morning.

The regulars were waiting in front of the door, shuffling from foot to foot with excitement. Josiah shoved the coffee into my hands. "Willa, you are quite the hero."

"Indeed," Hattie tittered. "So dangerous, so brave."

"Sheesh, give me a break." Pandora rolled her eyes. "*You* didn't have to deal with Fluff."

I ignored the cat. "I really didn't do much."

Cordelia waved her hand as they made their way to the sofa and chairs. "It's all over town how you captured Josie by hitting her on the head with *The Joy of Cooking*."

"Actually, it was Sarah that hit her with the book," I said.

"But it happened right here in your shop." Bing glanced around as if expecting to see a reenactment.

"Honestly, it really wasn't anything. It all kind of just happened. I didn't really do anything brave." I flushed, remembering how I'd actually tripped over Felicity in my attempts to stop Josie. If the regulars only knew what had really happened, Hattie and Cordelia's hair would turn whiter than it already was. The real hero had been Fluff, and I was glad he had only been momentarily knocked out and not really dead. Though he had looked quite dead when Felicity was holding him. I glanced at Pandora. Had she done something to bring him back? If she had, she didn't mention it to me.

"What about me?" Pandora sat at Bing's feet, staring up at him. He didn't answer because all he heard were meows. "I was the mastermind behind this."

I frowned down at her, and she smiled smugly. "Okay, I'll give you some of the credit too. I'm just glad it's all over with, and things are back to normal with my cat communication, and that I can still talk to my favorite human."

My heart melted at the compliment, and I smiled and made a note not to get so angry the next time she spooled the toilet paper off the roll or coughed up a hairball. Maybe I'd even spring for that expensive cat food.

"Did I read that Felicity Bates was here last night too?" Bing asked. "I didn't realize you two were friends."

Bing was staring at me intently. Did his words have some sort of double meaning? Bing had been involved in discovering that Felicity's son was a murderer. I got the impression he knew more than he let on about the secrets in Mystic Notch, but the other regulars seemed oblivious, so I didn't ask him. Maybe someday Bing and I would talk privately.

"I guess the article about Last Chance Books won't be printed in the Gazette now," Hattie said regrettably.

"Darn. I wanted to read all about it and possibly your mention of us regulars," Cordelia added.

"That is a shame," I said. "I said the loveliest things about you guys."

Dodged a bullet there.

"But did you hear about the new recipe contest in honor of Mary Ashford?" Hattie asked.

"No, I didn't. What's that about?"

"There's going to be an event in the town common next month," Hattie said.

"And there's a theme," Cordelia added.

"The post office has several notices about it pinned up already," Josiah said. "Of course, I won't be making anything, but I'd sure like to go and try out some samples."

Everyone laughed. "What is the theme?" I asked.

"Everyone needs to bake a dish related to a famous person from New Hampshire," Cordelia said.

"I'm doing Robert Frost." Hattie beamed with pride. "I can't tell you exactly what the dish is. It's a secret, and I don't want anyone to copy me."

Robert would be excited about that, but I didn't know how Franklin would feel about it. Probably jealous. Kind of odd that she picked Robert Frost out of all the potential people.

"What made you decide to do Robert Frost?" I asked.

"I'm not really sure. I just suddenly had an urge to do something in his name. I've gotten one of his biographies from your store here, and I happened to find something about one of his favorite dishes. That's what I'm making, and I'm going to name it after him."

Out of the corner of my eye, I saw a ghostly swirl over near the bookcase. It was Robert, beaming from ear to ear. Beside him, Franklin was frowning and staring intently at Cordelia.

"I'm going to do one too," Cordelia blurted out.

Hattie looked at her surprise. "I thought you said you didn't want to do any baking."

"I've suddenly changed my mind. I'm doing Franklin Pierce's presidential pizzelles."

Josiah leaned forward, his arms resting on his

thighs. "Is that a real thing? I don't remember anything about him eating Italian cookies."

"I think it is. I didn't make it up out of nowhere." Hattie glanced over to the exact spot where Franklin's ghost was standing. I knew she couldn't see him, but now I had to wonder if Franklin telepathed that message to her. I had no idea the ghosts could do that, which made me wonder if they'd ever done it to me.

"Well, all this talk about food and baking is making me hungry. I'm heading out to breakfast." Bing stood. "See you later, Willa."

"Yep, me too." Josiah stretched and tossed his Styrofoam coffee cup in the trash.

"We have to get home and check our pantry to see if we have the right ingredients for the contest." Hattie and Cordelia jumped up from their seat, and everyone headed out the door.

The regulars met Pepper on her way in. She was carrying a large mason jar filled with brown liquid—another tea.

"Willa! I'm so glad you're okay. I heard about the big arrest." She gave me an exaggerated wink since Hattie and Cordelia were still lingering in the doorway.

"Yes, it was all so odd how Josie ended up here," I said. "What do you have in your hand?"

I was a little dubious about having another tea steep in my window.

"This is a special tea, and I was hoping I could put it in your window to steep in the sun."

"Okay. But I'm sworn off teas."

Pepper laughed. "Well, I hope so. I don't want you to touch this one. It wards off unwanted attention, and if it backfires, it could bring too much attention."

Too much attention was the last thing I wanted. I shoved it way in the corner, and Pandora shifted to the side of her bed farthest from the jar and eyed it warily.

Pepper patted Pandora on the head. "Now, don't you go drinking this."

Pandora snorted. "No chance of that."

"What did she say?" Pepper asked me.

"She said no chance."

"I am glad, though, that you two can finally communicate." Pepper sounded sincere. "And that another threat has been removed from Mystic Notch."

"Those are good things, I suppose." I was still a little reluctant about my newfound belief in magic. I had fought it for a long time, but now it was clear that there was magic in the Notch, and apparently, I was part of it. It still felt a little funny though.

"I'm really proud of you, Willa." Pepper gave me an awkward hug. "Without you, things might not have turned out so good. And I know you resisted believing in magic for so long, but now you are coming into your own. Your grandmother would be proud."

I flushed with pride thinking of my grandmother. Come to think of it, she'd been best friends with Elspeth. The two had been tighter than peanut butter and jelly. My childhood days with the two of them had always seemed so magical. Had my grandmother actually been able to do magic?

I looked up at Pepper, and she nodded as if she'd read my mind. "Well, I have to run. Remember, don't touch that tea."

She rushed out the door, and Pandora and I both stared at the mason jar. We didn't need our newfound channel of communication to tell us that we were thinking the same thing. There was no way either one of us was touching that tea.

BY MIDAFTERNOON, I'D FINALLY SETTLED INTO MY regular routine and was entering some books into my inventory system on the computer when Pandora leapt out of her bed.

"Oh no! Close the shop and pretend we aren't here!" Her gaze was riveted on something outside the window.

"What? Why?" I looked out the window over her shoulder.

"They're coming!" She scrambled off her bed

and scurried into the back of the shop just as the door opened. Felicity Bates came in wearing a long lime-green dress with matching strappy sandals. Her red hair was sleek and shiny, pulled into an updo. Her fingernails were long and perfect, a pleasing shade of petal pink to match her toes. She looked like her old self. Maybe even better.

She was carrying a plate of cookies in one hand and the end of Fluff's pink leash in the other. Fluff looked pretty good too. His long white fur had been recently groomed and puffed about him like an ostrich boa. His tail was brushed out to four times its size. It looked like he had something in his mouth, but I couldn't tell what it was.

"I'm so glad I caught you, Willa," Felicity said as if I would be anywhere else.

She put the plate on the counter. "I hope you'll accept these homemade cookies. They're chocolate chip."

I did love chocolate chip cookies, but I was also suspicious of anything Felicity would bake for me. "You brought me cookies? Usually you just come in hurling insults."

"Not anymore." Felicity gestured toward her person. "I've fully recovered, and it's all thanks to you. And your darling cat, Pandora." She looked around. "Where is the little darling?"

Fluff was looking around too. Pandora trotted

cautiously out from the back. Apparently, her curiosity outweighed her dislike of the pair.

"Greetings," Pandora said.

"Mmm gy mimmm," Fluff mumbled.

"What did he say?" Pandora asked.

"I brought cookies for Willa, and Fluff brought something for you, Pandora," Felicity informed.

Fluff spit a limp mouse out on the floor at Pandora's feet. Gross!

Pandora didn't think it was so gross. She cocked her head, sniffed, and picked it up. "Thank you."

"Is that thing dead? You aren't going to eat it, are you? We should toss it out, could have a disease," I said to Pandora.

The cats ignored me.

Fluff bowed down in a downward dog stretch. "Your wish is my command."

Pandora wasn't impressed. "That's taking it a little far, isn't it?"

"Anyway, I just wanted to drop these off and see if there's anything you need." Felicity looked eager to please. "I could run an errand or maybe do your grocery shopping."

"I'm good. Thanks." Not only was I skeptical about her motives, but I really didn't want her doing any favors for me. "You don't have to come over and offer to do me favors just because of that portal thing."

"Oh yes, I do. I owe you, and I plan to pay my debt."

I glanced over at the tea Pepper had left. She'd said it would stop someone from getting too much attention, and apparently Felicity planned to give me lots of attention. But my interest in the tea was only fleeting. I'd seen what happened with the last one and several of her other teas. I wasn't desperate enough to risk it just yet.

"Oh, that's very nice. Thank you. Right now, all I need is to get back to my work." I pointed at my computer.

"Of course." Felicity looked like her feelings might be a little hurt. At least she could take a hint. She tugged on Fluff's leash and headed toward the door, hesitating with her hand on the knob. "Perhaps we could go to the spa together later?"

"Um, maybe." I stared at the door for a few seconds after she left. Hopefully her desire to be besties with me would wear off soon.

I looked down at Pandora, who had the mouse in her mouth. "Get rid of that disgusting thing."

"It's not disgusting. It's a nice gift." Pandora dropped it, and to my surprise, the little thing shook itself off and ran toward the front door.

"For a minute there I thought you were going to eat it."

"The mouse? Nah. It's a living creature. He can

fit under the door and go about his business now. Speaking of eating, I want to put in an order."

"An order?"

"Yeah. Next time you go grocery shopping, can you pick up some of that premium wet cat food? The stuff with the gravy. Turkey and salmon if they have it. Oh! And maybe some lobster meat? Pretty please?"

I stared down at the cat. Is this how it was going to be now? Grocery orders? Lobster? Next she'd be picking out cat beds online and demanding special grooming sessions.

In the last few days, things sure had changed for me. I just wasn't sure how many of those changes were for the better.

****

Sign up for my newsletter and get my latest releases at the lowest discount price, plus I'll send you a link for a free download of a book in one of my other series: https://mysticnotch.gr8.com

Books in the Mystic Notch series:
Ghostly Paws
A Spirited Tail
A Mew To A Kill
Paws and Effect

Probable Paws
A Whisker of a Doubt
Wrong Side of the Claw
Claw and Order

Join my readers group on Facebook:
https://www.facebook.com/groups/ldobbsreaders

A Whisker of a Doubt

Wrong Side of the Claw

Claw and Order

Juniper Holiday Cozy Mysteries

***

Halloween Party Murder

Thanksgiving Dinner Death

Who Slayed The Santas?

Masquerade Party Murder

My Fatal Valentine

Oyster Cove Guesthouse

Cat Cozy Mystery Series

***

A Twist in the Tail

A Whisker in the Dark

A Purrfect Alibi

Kate Diamond Mystery Adventures

***

Hidden Agemda (Book 1)

Ancient Hiss Story (Book 2)

Heist Society (Book 3)

Silver Hollow

Paranormal Cozy Mystery Series

***

A Spell of Trouble (Book 1)

Spell Disaster (Book 2)

Nothing to Croak About (Book 3)

Cry Wolf (Book 4)

Shear Magic (Book 5)

Mooseamuck Island

Cozy Mystery Series

* * *

A Zen For Murder

A Crabby Killer

A Treacherous Treasure

Blackmoore Sisters

Cozy Mystery Series

* * *

Dead Wrong

Dead & Buried

Dead Tide

Buried Secrets

Deadly Intentions

A Grave Mistake

Spell Found

Fatal Fortune

Hidden Secrets

Lexy Baker

Cozy Mystery Series

* * *

Killer Cupcakes

Dying For Danish

Murder, Money and Marzipan

3 Bodies and a Biscotti

Brownies, Bodies & Bad Guys

Bake, Battle & Roll

Wedded Blintz

Scones, Skulls & Scams

Ice Cream Murder

Mummified Meringues

Brutal Brulee (Novella)

No Scone Unturned

Cream Puff Killer

Never Say Pie

Ain't Seen Muffin Yet

Assault and Buttercream

Lady Katherine Regency Mysteries

***

An Invitation to Murder (Book 1)

The Baffling Burglaries of Bath (Book 2)

Murder at the Ice Ball (Book 3)

A Murderous Affair (Book 4)

Murder on Charles Street (Book 5)

Julia and Nora Marsh 1920s Cozy Mystery

***

Murder on a Mississippi Steamboat

Hazel Martin Historical Mystery Series

***

Murder at Lowry House (book 1)

Murder by Misunderstanding (book 2)

Sam Mason Mysteries

(As L. A. Dobbs)

***

Telling Lies (Book 1)

Keeping Secrets (Book 2)

Exposing Truths (Book 3)

Betraying Trust (Book 4)

Killing Dreams (Book 5)

More books in the Rockford Security Series:

Cold As Her Heart

A Game of Kill

No One To Trust

No Time To Run

Don't Fear The Truth

Hide From The Past

Romantic Comedy

***

Corporate Chaos Series

In Over Her Head (book 1)

Can't Stand the Heat (book 2)

What Goes Around Comes Around (book 3)

Careful What You Wish For (4)

Dish Best Served Cold (5)

Contemporary Romance

***

Reluctant Romance

Sweet Romance (Written As Annie Dobbs)

Firefly Inn Series

***

Another Chance (Book 1)

Another Wish (Book 2)

Hometown Hearts Series

***

No Getting Over You (Book 1)

A Change of Heart (Book 2)

Sweet Mountain Billionaires

***

Jaded Billionaire (Book 1)

A Billion Reasons Not To Fall In Love (Book 2)

***

Sweetrock Sweet and Spicy Cowboy Romance

Some Like It Hot

Too Close For Comfort

————

Regency Romance

* * *

Scandals and Spies Series:

Kissing The Enemy

Deceiving the Duke

Tempting the Rival

Charming the Spy

Pursuing the Traitor

Captivating the Captain

The Unexpected Series:

An Unexpected Proposal

An Unexpected Passion

Dobbs Fancytales:

Dobbs Fancytales Boxed Set Collection

———

Western Historical Romance

***

Goldwater Creek Mail Order Brides:

Faith

American Mail Order Brides Series:

Chevonne: Bride of Oklahoma

————————

Magical Romance with a Touch of Mystery

***

Something Magical

Curiously Enchanted

ABOUT THE AUTHOR

Leighann Dobbs discovered her passion for writing after a twenty year career as a software engineer. She lives in New Hampshire with her husband Bruce, their trusty Chihuahua mix Mojo and beautiful rescue cat, Kitty. When she's not reading, gardening or selling antiques, she likes to write romance and cozy mystery novels and novelettes which are perfect for the busy person on the go.

Sign up for her newsletter and get her latest releases at the lowest discount price, plus a free copy of **Dead Wrong**, book 1 in the award winning paranormal Blackmoore Sisters Paranormal Cozy Mystery Series: https://mysticnotch.gr8.com

Connect with Leighann on Facebook and Twitter
http://facebook.com/leighanndobbsbooks

This is a work of fiction.

None of it is real. All names, places, and events are products of the author's imagination. Any resemblance to real names, places, or events are purely coincidental, and should not be construed as being real.

CLAW AND ORDER

Copyright © 2021

Leighann Dobbs Publishing

http://www.leighanndobbs.com

All Rights Reserved.

No part of this work may be used or reproduced in any manner, except as allowable under "fair use," without the express written permission of the author.

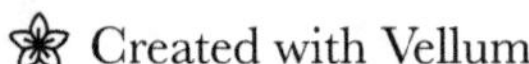 Created with Vellum

9 781946 944894